HER SHADOW

Slick Rock 5

Becca Van

MENAGE EVERLASTING

Siren Publishing, Inc.
www.SirenPublishing.com

A SIREN PUBLISHING BOOK
IMPRINT: Ménage Everlasting

HER SHADOW MEN
Copyright © 2012 by Becca Van

ISBN: 978-1-62241-151-1

First Printing: July 2012

Cover design by Les Byerley
All art and logo copyright © 2012 by Siren Publishing, Inc.

Printed in the U.S.A.

PUBLISHER
Siren Publishing, Inc.
www.SirenPublishing.com

DEDICATION

To all the men and women serving our countries and risking their lives to keep our world safe. Thank you from the bottom of my heart.

HER SHADOW MEN

Slick Rock 5

BECCA VAN
Copyright © 2012

Chapter One

Debbie Newsome felt the hair on the back of her neck prickle and stand on end. She had been working quietly in her new lingerie store, hanging new stock on racks, until she felt eyes upon her. She turned around slowly and peered out her shop's front window. She couldn't see anyone, but the sensation of being watched sent shivers racing up and down her spine. She wished she had put blinds on her windows so she could pull them down until she was ready to unlock the front door for potential customers. This wasn't the first time she had felt as if someone was watching her. The sensation gave her the willies.

She wondered if it was Britt and Daniel Delaney watching her again. She had met the two handsome men through Debbie's new friend Leah. But Debbie had vowed she was off men for the rest of her life.

Debbie sighed as she turned back to the racks. She had embarrassed herself when she had begged Connell and Seamus O'Hara, who were now Leah's husbands, to take her back. She had finally decided she was ready for a committed relationship, but she was too late. Leah had already had the two men panting after her.

She knew she hadn't really been in love with Connell and Seamus, but she felt life was passing her by. She had felt the tick of her maternal clock beating inside her and wanted to start a family. That wasn't going to happen now. She would have to be happy with her new business and the upstairs apartment she lived in.

Debbie glanced at the clock and sighed again. It was time to open the doors for business. She walked over and unlocked the entry, glancing up and down the street and waving to some other business owners as they opened their stores.

She smiled when she saw Leah coming toward the shop. Her friend was glowing with health from her pregnancy, and she could see the small baby bump under her shirt.

"Hi, Leah. How are you feeling?"

"I'm great," her friend replied, patting her stomach. "But I need some new bras. I can't believe I've outgrown these ones already."

"I guess that's normal. Do you mind if I get a coffee while you look? I haven't had a chance to breathe all morning," Debbie stated with a smile.

"You go right ahead, honey. I'll just browse until you come back out."

Debbie got her coffee and was back moments later. She watched as Leah took a heap of lingerie into the dressing room to try it all on. Debbie sat at her counter and sipped at her coffee as she perused lingerie stock online. She looked up when the bell tinkled and felt nervous flutters in her stomach. Her pussy clenched at the sight of Britt and Daniel Delaney walking into her shop. She wondered what they wanted because she knew they weren't here to buy anything.

"Hi, Debbie. How's business?" Britt asked.

Debbie's sheath clenched and dripped at the sound of Britt's deep, gravelly voice. She shifted on her stool, trying to keep her face expressionless, and answered him coolly.

"Booming. I'm going to have to hire an employee soon. Can I help you with anything?"

"Yes, as a matter of fact you can, Debbie," Daniel replied. "Come to dinner with us tonight."

"No, thanks. I'm too busy."

"You have to eat, darlin'. Surely it won't make much difference whether you stay home or spend an hour with us, sharing a meal," Britt suggested.

"Sorry, I have too much to do. I do the paperwork while I'm eating dinner. Look, I appreciate the offer but I'm just not interested," Debbie lied.

She looked from Britt to Daniel and felt her breasts swell and her nipples harden. What was it about these two men that got to her? Sure, they were sexy, handsome men, but she had seen those before and not reacted. Britt was a very tall, muscular man. He stood at least six foot six, and his shoulders were the widest she had ever seen. He had sandy-blond hair and blue eyes. His eyelashes were so long they curled up at the ends. It was such a sinful waste for a man to have such beautiful lashes. He had such beautiful eyelashes, but they didn't detract from his rugged, he-man sort of handsomeness. His muscles bunched and bulged as he moved, and she knew he would have no trouble picking her up if he wished to.

Daniel wasn't as tall as his brother, but he was still a hell of a lot taller than her height of five foot seven. He had to be around six foot three, and he had black hair and green eyes. His face was less rugged but no less appealing. He was more classically handsome than his sibling, and his build, though solid and muscular, was sleeker than Britt's. She drew her eyes back up to Britt's and saw his lips tilt up at the corners. She hoped he hadn't seen how they affected her.

Debbie sighed with relief as Leah walked out of the dressing room. She averted her face from the two brothers and stood up to take Leah's purchases.

"Hi, Britt, Daniel, how are you?" Leah asked.

"We're fine, Leah. How are you and the baby?" Daniel asked.

"We're good. Oh hey, we're having a barbecue tonight. Why don't you come on out and share a meal with us? You, too, Debbie," Leah offered, and Debbie saw the sly smile she directed toward her.

"Thanks, Leah. That would be great. What time do you want us there?" Daniel asked.

"Seven would be perfect," Leah replied.

"Okay. We'll pick you up around six thirty, Debbie," Daniel stated.

"Oh but—"

"I'm looking forward to it, Leah. We'll see you tonight," Britt said, and he and Daniel left with a wave before Debbie could reply.

"I hate you," Debbie said as she turned to glare at Leah.

"No you don't. Come on, Deb. You know those two men get your motor revving. What harm can it do to come out to the ranch and share some food?" Leah asked.

"None," Debbie replied reluctantly. "I'm just not sure I want to get involved with anyone, Leah. You were nearly killed because of me and I made a fool of myself over your husbands. I'm just not ready to start another relationship."

"Who said you had to? Why not just have a fling with them? They're good men, Debbie. They would never hurt you intentionally," Leah stated.

"That's what I'm worried about. Intentional or not, I just know I'll end up getting hurt again. I'm not sure I want to put myself up for pain. I've been there before. I think it would be best if I just stayed home."

"And what are you going to do? More work, I'll bet. Come on, Debbie. Please come and have dinner with us, for me?"

"God, you're such a bitch. You know I can't refuse you when you use those puppy-dog eyes on me. All right. There. Are you satisfied? But don't go trying to push me onto those two men. It won't work out, and I'm not willing to take the chance," Debbie said firmly.

"I wouldn't dream of it," Leah replied.

Debbie finished ringing up Leah's purchases and waved her friend good-bye. She just knew Leah was going to do her damnedest to get her with the two Delaney brothers. Well, she was made of sterner stuff than that. She wasn't about to give in to her friend's matchmaking.

* * * *

By the time Debbie closed the door and locked up, she was exhausted. She was definitely going to have to hire someone to help out in the store. She turned off the lights and headed for the stairs off the back door. The stairs to her apartment ran on the outside of the building. She was glad no one could access her home from the inside of her shop.

After Debbie showered, she stood wrapped in a towel as she contemplated the contents of her wardrobe. She pulled out her little black dress and then shoved it back into the closet. She wasn't going to make any effort to look nice. She was just going to a cookout for goodness' sake. She pulled out her favorite pair of worn jeans and a purple shirt. She loved purple, and her closet was rife in various shades of the color. She pulled her clothes on over her violet lacy camisole and G-string, then brushed her hair once more. Instead of putting it up in her usual hair clip, she let the blonde tresses fall over her shoulders and down her back. She had always loved having long hair. Her hair was her one true vanity, and she had vowed, other than the occasional trim, she would leave it as it was.

Debbie slipped her feet into a pair of sandals and walked to the kitchen. She jumped when a she heard a knock on her door. She walked to the entry, took a couple of deep breaths as she wiped her sweaty palms on her black jeans, and opened the door. Her heart did a flip-flop in her chest to see Britt standing outside on the small landing.

"Wow, you look great, Deb. Are you ready to go? Can I help you with anything?"

"Um, no. I'm good, just a second," Deb said and turned back into her apartment. She grabbed her purse and the large bowl of potato salad she'd bought from the deli.

"Let me take that for you, darlin'," Britt said and took the bowl out of her hands. Debbie stepped out onto the landing and pulled the door closed behind her. She locked the dead bolt and turned to see Britt staring at her. She glanced away quickly, not wanting to get caught up in his sexy blue eyes. Debbie started down the stairs and shivered. When she glanced back she saw Britt's eyes on her ass. She couldn't seem to stop herself from putting an extra sway in her hips. She turned toward the sound of an engine and saw Daniel behind the wheel of a large dual-cab truck idling in the alley.

Daniel was out of the truck by the time she got to the back door. He opened it for her and then lifted her up to the seat with ease. Debbie turned her head toward him and hoped the heated skin of her cheeks weren't as red as they felt.

"Thank you."

"Anytime, honey. Here, let me buckle you in," Daniel stated and reached over her for the safety belt.

Debbie couldn't contain the shiver running through her body when Daniel's large, bulging bicep brushed against her breasts. She felt her nipples pucker and mentally cursed her body's reaction. Her pussy clenched as she looked up into Daniel's green, heated stare. She wanted to unbuckle her belt and jump his bones, but instead she looked down at her hands which were clenched in her lap. She sighed with relief when he closed the door quietly and walked around to get into the driver's seat.

She looked out the window as they drove along. Colorado was such beautiful country. The fields were strewn with spring wildflowers. The grass was green, and crops were bountiful. She cracked her window and breathed in the scent of primrose and mown grass. She had always loved the colors and scents of spring and autumn.

"You're pretty quiet, darlin'. Are you okay?" Britt asked.

Debbie looked up to see Britt turned toward her from the front seat.

"Yes, thanks. I'm just tired. It was a long day."

"You really should think about hiring on some help. You're going to run yourself ragged if you try to do everything yourself all the time," Britt stated.

"I know. I was going to work on an advertisement tonight. I'll have to do it in the morning. How long are you two staying in town?"

"We've bought our own place just outside of town. We are going to be working with the sheriff and deputies in this town. The crime rate is picking up since the population has begun expanding so rapidly," Britt replied.

"I thought you worked in a special-operatives branch for the government. Won't you need to live in the city to be on hand?"

"We still work for the government, honey. It doesn't matter where we live. We can be where we need to within hours," Daniel explained.

"So are you both sheriffs now?"

"No, darlin', we're deputy marshals," Britt answered.

"Oh. Your work must be pretty dangerous," Debbie commented.

"Well, I suppose you could say that. But we have had years of elite training. We know what we're doing, darlin," Britt stated.

Debbie didn't reply. What they did for a living shouldn't matter to her. Her heart shouldn't clench at the thought of them being in danger, either. But once again she couldn't seem to stop herself.

She looked up as Daniel slowed the truck and turned into the drive for the ranch. She knew Britt and Daniel were as attracted to her as she was to them. She was just going to have to be strong. There was no way she was letting them into her life or her bed. Her shop was going to come first, and she was going to learn to be content living alone. She told herself that she didn't need a man or men in her life to feel fulfilled, but as soon as the thought passed through her mind, she knew it was a lie.

She pushed her musings away and got out of the truck as soon as Daniel pulled up. She was at the back door of the house before Britt and Daniel even got out of the truck.

Chapter Two

"Hi, Debbie, come on in," Seamus said as he held the door open for her.

Debbie exchanged greetings with Seamus, Connell, and Leah as she entered the kitchen.

"Damn, I forgot to bring in the potato salad," Debbie muttered and turned, only to bump up against a large male body.

"I've got it, honey," Daniel said, and she tried not to tense up when he placed a hand at her elbow to steady her. "It looks and smells delicious, Debbie."

"It's nothing special," Debbie said with a shrug and moved away, but he followed her.

"You smell real nice, honey."

Debbie lowered her head when she felt heat in her cheeks. She didn't know how to respond to compliments. Sure, men had flattered her before, but she still didn't know how to handle them. She kept her eyes to the floor and prayed for someone to take the attention off of her.

"Deb, can you give me a hand taking out the salads? We're eating out on the deck," Leah stated.

"Sure," Deb replied and hurried over to Leah's side. Once the table was set and the men were in their element at the grill, Deb accepted the glass of wine Leah offered. Only after she took a sip did she remember her friend was pregnant.

"I forgot you wouldn't be drinking. Sorry, Leah, I should have thought."

"What do you have to be sorry for? You didn't make me pregnant," Leah stated then burst into laughter. Deb couldn't help but laugh as well. "Just drink up and enjoy."

Debbie was more than happy to do so. As soon as she sat down she felt the day's work lift from her.

"I'm going to place an ad in the local paper tomorrow, to hire someone on," Debbie told Leah.

"Girl, you have the one and only lingerie store in town. Of course business is booming. Women love to know they can pick out pretty lingerie to wear. It's about time you hired someone to help you out. You need to have some down time so you don't burn out."

"Yeah, I guess. I just didn't expect to do so well since I'm new in town. I thought it would take months before I started making any profit. I can't believe how well the shop is doing."

"You set up a shop which was needed. I'm not surprised, Deb. Congratulations and may you keep reaping the rewards," Leah said and toasted Debbie with her glass of orange juice.

"Leah, I need a plate to put the steak and ribs on when they're cooked. Can you get me one please?" Connell called.

"I'll get it, you sit and relax," Debbie declared.

"Thanks, it's in the cupboard above the oven," Leah said.

Debbie pulled the large platter from the cupboard and turned her head when she felt large hands at her waist. She looked up into Britt's blue eyes.

"What do you want?" she asked as she turned to face him. Britt pulled the plate from her hands and set it on the counter behind him. He placed his hand back on her waist and stared down at her. Then he slowly lifted her off her feet until she was almost at eye level with him. She clutched at his shoulders, and instinctively her legs wrapped around his waist to hold her against his form.

"This," Britt replied, and then his mouth was on hers. His lips were so soft and warm. He didn't come on too strong. He brushed his flesh across hers, and she felt his tongue lick over her lips.

Debbie couldn't prevent a moan from escaping as she opened to him. He wrapped an arm around her waist and the other beneath her ass as he supported her weight while he devoured her mouth. She clung to his shoulders and slid her tongue along his. Her breasts ached with need, and she rubbed her nipples on his chest through her clothes, trying to ease the tension. He kissed her again and again, tasting every inch of her mouth. She knew she should stop him and pull away, but she couldn't seem to find the strength to do so.

She gasped into his mouth when she felt another pair of hands slide around her from behind, and then her nipples were being pinched. She tightened her legs around Britt and began to rock her hips against his straining cock. She wasn't even aware of her shirt and bra being undone until warm fingers touched her naked nipples. She mewed when Britt thrust against her, the head of his denim-covered cock rubbing on her cloth-covered clit. She sobbed into his mouth, her limbs shaking as she climaxed for the first time in over two years.

The hands at her breasts eased away and slid around to her back. When her bra was done up, those hands soothed her back, belly, and waist with soft caresses.

Britt had slowed the kiss, and he removed his lips from hers. She stared up into his blue eyes and felt her cheeks heat with shame. God, she had just come in her best friend's kitchen. *What the hell is wrong with me?* She lowered her gaze, and removed her legs from around Britt's waist. He eased her down to the floor and held her until she was steady. Debbie was so embarrassed that she couldn't think of a single thing to say to him. She did the only thing she could think of, which was to pick up the platter and dart outside. She didn't dare look back to see Britt's reaction.

She had just led two men on without meaning to. Now they were going to think she was an easy lay. That certainly wasn't the case. She'd only ever had three men in her life. The first was her crazy ex, and then there had been Connell and Seamus, who had loved her together.

She knew now she had been too young and immature to note the difference between infatuation and love. She wished she could turn back the clock and still be a virgin.

She took the plate over to Connell and sat down beside Leah. There was no way she was giving Britt and Daniel room to put the moves on her again. Not if she could help it.

"Are you all right, Debbie? You look a little flushed," Leah observed.

"I'm fine. This is really nice wine, Leah. What is it?" Debbie asked, trying to divert the conversation's track.

"Debbie, you're going to have to face the fact you are attracted to those two men. You can lie to yourself as much as you want, but we both know you are going to end up in their arms and their bed," Leah said quietly. "Besides, from all the moaning I heard you doing I'd say they've already half succeeded."

"Oh God. You heard that?" Debbie asked, looking up to see Leah smiling at her. She cringed when her friend nodded.

"Did your men hear, too?"

"No, honey, just me. So did they get you off, or did they just kiss you?"

"Leah, you are incorrigible," Debbie whispered.

"Well, that answers that question. I don't really need to ask the next one."

"What's that?"

"I was going to ask if it was any good, but I know from the sounds you were making it was. Oh, oh, here they come. Ooh, they look so determined and they're staring right at you. Girl, you don't stand a chance."

Debbie just shot Leah a glare and looked down at her hands, once again clenched in her lap. She sighed and let her tense muscles relax when Daniel and Britt walked over to the grill. She could hear the men laughing and joking as they stood around the grill. It wasn't long before the four men walked back toward the table, the cooked meat on the platter.

"I forgot the dinner rolls, I'll be back in a moment," Leah said and hurried into the house before Debbie could do it for her. She looked up at Connell and Seamus and smiled as they sat down across from her. She couldn't help but tense up again when Britt and Daniel sat on either side of her, but she didn't look at them. Debbie tried to ignore the two brothers, but it was impossible. As they all sat around eating and talking, Britt and Daniel plied her with questions. It would have been rude of her to ignore them totally. So she decided to keep her answers short and sweet without any emotion in her voice.

When the meal was over, Debbie helped Leah clean up, load the dishwasher, and make the coffee. By the time they had finished she was so tired she could hardly keep her eyes open. Britt, Daniel, and Debbie said their thank-yous and good-byes.

In the car, Debbie leaned her head back against the seat headrest. She was glad tomorrow was Saturday and she only had a half day to work at the shop. Sunday, she planned to sleep until she woke naturally, without the piercing shriek of her alarm. She had always been an early riser, but felt like she could sleep for a week.

She must have drifted off because the next thing she knew, Britt was leaning over her unbuckling her seat belt. She looked up at him through sleep-hazed eyes and couldn't help but smile at him. He was so sexy, and even though she should work at keeping him and his brother at arm's length, she was failing miserably.

Britt helped her out of the truck and placed an arm around her waist. He guided her up the stairs to her apartment and waited while she rummaged in her purse for her key. She was about to place the key in her lock, but Britt took it from her hand and did it for her and opened her door.

"Thank you. Good night," Debbie said and took a step away from him. She didn't get very far. He wrapped an arm around her waist, turned her to face him, bent down, and took her lips with a kiss so gentle and tender it brought tears to her eyes. She blinked and looked away, only to connect with Daniel's green eyes. He took her by the shoulders and kissed her, too. By the time the kiss was over, her pussy clenched and her clit throbbed. She walked into her apartment and began to close the door.

"Don't think this is over, Debbie. We've only just started," Britt stated, and she could see by the determination in his eyes that he wasn't about to let her push him and his brother away. She closed the door, shot the bolt, and leaned against the timber. Without a physical barrier to keep them apart, she didn't know if she had the will or the strength to push them away.

Chapter Three

As his brother pulled into the driveway, Britt realized he had spent the entire car ride home lost in his fantasies of Debbie and their encounter in the kitchen. Daniel put the car in park and looked across the cab of the truck. Britt met his brother's gaze and saw his own desires reflected back at him.

Britt confessed what he had been thinking for the entire ride home. "God, she's such a sexy little thing. My dick is so hard and I swear my balls are turning blue already." Wincing, he adjusted his cock.

"Yes, she is." Clearly lost in his own fantasy, Daniel stared out the windshield toward the darkened house. "I could just drown in those pretty eyes of hers. They go so dark and stormy when she's turned on. I can't believe you made her come and you didn't even have her naked. I can't wait to get my mouth on that sweet, creamy pussy of hers."

Recalling the way Debbie had fled the kitchen, Britt shook his head. "She's going to fight us. She's wary and nervous, but she wants us too. She was embarrassed after I made her come so easily. She could hardly look me in the eye," Britt explained.

"I think she's commitment shy. You and I both know what her ex was like. After him, she went out with Leah's husbands, but Seamus told me that was over two years ago. That didn't work out either."

"Yeah, she has a commitment phobia all right. But, man, did she eat you up with her eyes when you weren't looking at her," Britt said. He smiled to himself. "At least she knows how a ménage works. We won't have to be worried about her running scared on account of that."

Daniel continued to gaze out the windshield, and Britt wondered if his brother was even listening. "I love it when she leaves her hair down. God, that hair is so wild, with all those blonde waves and kinks. Those eyes of hers turn dark gray when she's aroused. I'll bet she wears the sexiest lingerie we can imagine. I wish we could have stripped her down in that kitchen and touched her sweet-smelling skin," Daniel rasped. "Shit, we've got to change the subject. It's getting downright painful sitting here with my cock so hard it's aching."

"Yeah, I hear you, brother." Britt opened the passenger door. They'd sat here long enough, and he wanted to clear his head. "I'm going to see what we have from the agency. There's been a lot of criminal activity lately. I don't like it. I feel like something big is going down, but until we have our next assignment we just have to sit pretty. I guess that'll give us more time to work on our woman."

Daniel only nodded. It seemed as though his thoughts were still being pulled that direction. Britt decided to give him a minute alone.

Britt was inside the house making a pot of coffee before he heard Daniel enter. He looked up to see his brother reaching for two coffee mugs. It was going to be a long night. Once he had a full mug in his hand, Britt went to the study while Daniel turned on the TV. He booted up his computer and listened to the messages on the answering machine. Most of them were just friends and family touching base, but the last message made him sit up straight in his chair. It was from the head of the agency, and he didn't like what he heard one little bit.

Fuck. He didn't need to have to deal with this shit right now. He wanted to concentrate on getting Debbie into his bed. He sighed and rose to feet. He needed to talk to his brother.

"What's up?" Daniel asked as soon as he entered the room.

Britt and Daniel were more in tune with each other than most brothers. They had gone through an elite training program with nearly all aspects of the military and were third *dan* black belts in karate.

They could lose themselves amongst shadows and become nearly invisible to the human eye. They had learned their trade well and were that good at hiding.

They could move with speed and stealth and were lightning fast when necessary. They had made up their own language using hand signals and facial expressions. Just the twitch of an eyebrow could mean the difference between life and death. They worked out regularly, pushing their bodies to the limit of their strength and endurance, but it was all necessary if they were to survive pitting themselves against the evil in the world.

"We have a problem. That bomber we put away a few years back has managed to escape from prison. He's as good as announced he's headed for us," Britt stated and took a seat on the sofa.

"Do you mean Glen Parker?"

"Yeah." Britt rubbed his face. The news of the breakout was unwelcome, but now that Parker was out, it was no surprise that the man was heading for them. Britt still remembered Parker shouting "Like for like" across the courtroom at them. He blamed Britt and Daniel for the loss of his family, and he had promised he would get the Delaneys back.

"Fuck. How the hell would he know where we are? We never use credit cards to travel, we always use cash," Daniel said, his frustration apparent.

"We just bought a house, Dan. How hard would it be to find our names in the town records?"

"How long has he been on the run?"

"A couple of days."

"Shit. Do you think he had inside help to find us? It would have taken a lot longer to find us without it," Daniel said.

"That's what I was thinking, but I don't think so. As far as anyone around here knows we are just deputy marshals. The other operatives wouldn't sell anyone out. Parker must have had access to a computer while he was in prison. He probably did a search on our names and they came up because of our property purchase," Britt speculated.

"Wait a minute. Didn't Debbie know we were some sort of some sort of government operatives? How the hell could she have known that?" Daniel asked.

"No way, Dan. She had nothing to do with it. She probably got her information from Leah. Seamus and Connell knew who we worked for. We told them when Leah was in trouble."

"Shit, I know. I didn't really think she had sold us out. I'm just grasping at straws." Daniel paused as though realizing something. "God, we are going to have to keep an eye on Debbie. If this guy comes to town, she is going to be in danger because of us. Glen Parker is one mean son of a bitch."

"I know. I'll call Sheriff Luke Sun-Walker and Damon Osborne. I'll have them keep an eye out for anyone new to town, just in case he's not working alone. I'll also send him a photo of the bastard. There's not much we can do but watch over her," Britt stated.

"Oh, I don't know about that. I want her living here with us. The sooner she's in our house and our bed I will feel so much better," Daniel said.

"I will, too, Dan. But you and I both know that's not going to happen for a while. She's going to baulk every time we get near her."

"But she will give in eventually. As much as I know she wants to resist us, I'm not sure she can," Daniel replied with a smile.

"From now on, I think one of us should take her lunch every day. She'll get used to us being around faster," Britt declared.

"Good idea. I'll go first," Daniel pronounced. Despite the circumstances and the dangers that might lie ahead, he shot Britt a grin. "I missed out when you two were in the kitchen. It's my turn."

Chapter Four

"Thank you," Debbie said to her customer. "I hope to see you again soon." She glanced at her watch. It was only 11:30 a.m., but it felt like it should be four in the afternoon. She couldn't believe how busy she had been this morning. Already her feet were sore and her lower back was aching.

She'd had a constant stream of customers, and since she hadn't slept well, she was having trouble coping with the workload. Since starting work at seven, she had written up an advertisement to hire on some help, updated her expenditures and sales, and placed another order for more lingerie. She had never been more relieved for it to be Saturday, and she couldn't wait to be able to close her doors at two this afternoon. By the end of the week she was usually exhausted, and the reduced hours at the start of the weekend were her only way of coping. If she got someone to answer that ad, relief would be in sight. That way she could do the dreaded necessary paperwork during working hours instead of before or after.

Taking advantage of the lull between customers, she went to the kitchen and poured herself a coffee. She took a sip then sighed when she heard the bell over the door calling her. She hesitated when she saw Daniel Delaney walking toward the counter, but tried to school her expression into a polite, cool mask.

"Hi, honey, how are you?" Daniel asked.

"I'm fine, thank you. What brings you here?"

"You do, of course. I brought you some lunch," Daniel replied.

He lifted his hand to show her a bag from the diner, and her stomach growled at the thought of the good food inside. She hadn't taken the time to eat breakfast that morning, and seeing that bag had her salivating.

She made her way around the sales counter and sat down on the stool. She watched as Daniel placed the sack before her and then pushed it toward her.

"Why don't you eat while you have your coffee? I'll keep you company," Daniel stated and gave her a wink.

"What do you want, Daniel? I don't have time to waste. I'm too busy."

"You work too hard. Will it really hurt you to take a few minutes to eat and relax? You have no customers at the moment. Eat. You look tired. When are you going to hire in for some help?"

"I placed an ad in the paper this morning. Thank you for lunch," Debbie added and reached for the bag. The scent of the veggie sandwich caused her mouth to salivate and her stomach to growl again.

"It looks like I was just in time." He smiled at her and watched her take her first bite. Even though Debbie felt nervous and self-conscious in his presence, she was too hungry to argue with him. She hadn't even realized she had been hungry until he had walked through the door. She sipped her coffee when the sandwich was gone and realized she was being rude.

"Would you like a cup of coffee?"

"Yes, that would be nice."

Debbie was about to rise to get it when the door opened, admitting a customer.

"You attend to your customer. I can get myself a coffee," Daniel said and then walked across the room and disappeared into her small kitchen.

Debbie pushed him from her mind and got to work. By the time the customer left with two bags full of underwear and happy smile, Debbie had forgotten Daniel was in the back. She was too busy to even think. She worked diligently for the next two hours and then sighed as she turned the *closed* sign on the shop door. She bolted the dead bolt and sighed as she went back to the counter to slump over it. Her feet, legs, and back were killing her.

Large hands settled at her waist. Debbie jumped and squeaked with surprise. She looked over her shoulder and straightened up when she saw Daniel looming over her.

"Sorry, honey, I didn't mean to scare you," Daniel said as he stepped back.

"What are you still doing here? I thought you had already left."

"I don't know whether to be insulted or not," Daniel said and gave her a smirk. "I have been looking over your security system and locks. They're not good enough, honey. You need to get a better system, and the lock on your apartment door would be child's play to get through."

"Excuse me? What gives you the right to go snooping around my store and apartment? I can't believe you did that. And stop calling me 'honey.' I have a name, use it," Deb said through clenched teeth. *How dare he do this to her? Who did he think he was?*

"I didn't go into your apartment, Deb. I was just making sure you have the right security. You never know when you will need it. I don't like the fact that you are living alone and could be vulnerable to criminals. I was just trying to help. I know what I'm talking about. I have spent years fighting scumbags and criminals. I just want to know you're safe."

"Then I suggest you take it up with the security company. I got what I could afford at the time, Daniel. I don't care what you think or say. I have security and I won't be forking out any more money for more. Nearly every penny I earn goes back into this business and now I am going to hire some help I will also be paying a wage. So just back off."

"Hey, don't go getting touchy. I was only concerned for your welfare," Daniel replied calmly.

"Please, leave. I have too much to do to waste time talking to you."

"Ouch. Okay, but don't think you've seen the last of us, Deb. We like you a lot and we mean to have you in our bed," Daniel stated.

Debbie watched until he walked over to the door, unlocked it, and exited. He turned back to her and pinned her with his heated stare. "Lock up after me," he said, and then he was gone.

"In your dreams, pal," Debbie muttered under her breath. She locked up, glanced out onto the street through the glass, and watched Daniel until he disappeared around the corner. *God, woman, you are so pathetic. You can't even take your eyes off him when he's walking away.*

Debbie spent a couple of hours doing her sales report, and then she headed upstairs to her apartment. She cleaned her one bedroom from top to bottom, and by the time she had finished she was so tired she was hardly able to stay on her feet. She stripped off her clothes, showered, and fell into bed. Her last thought as she drifted off was of Britt and Daniel.

* * * *

Debbie came awake fully alert. She glanced at her glowing alarm clock and saw it was just after midnight. She listened intently, wondering what had awakened her from such a deep sleep. She didn't hear anything other than the normal creaks and groans as the timber frame of her building cooled and contracted. Something crashed downstairs, and she bolted upright. Her heart began pounding rapidly in her chest, her palms became sweaty, and her breathing escalated. The sound had come from her store.

She got out of bed and pulled on jeans and a sweater. She didn't stop to think about what she was doing. She crept out of her apartment and down the stairs. The back door to her shop was open.

Slipping back upstairs, she grabbed the softball bat she kept on hand for safety and her cell phone.

It was too dark to see. Controlling the trembling in her fingers, she punched in 9-1-1 but hesitated before pressing the *call* button. She wanted to see what was happening first. With the bat secure in her hands and her phone in her pocket, she went back downstairs.

The next thump convinced her that someone was definitely in the store. Probably a thief, she thought. The idea that someone was stealing her merchandise set off her temper. Emboldened by her outrage, she moved silently to the doorway between the kitchen and the shop. She peered around the corner and held her breath. She saw the shadow of a large man at her cash register. It looked like he was trying to pry the cash drawer open. She was thankful she took most of her cash from her register every night, but there was still some left in the drawer. She moved quietly and was nearly on the intruder when he looked up.

Debbie let out an almighty yell and swung her bat with everything she had. The bastard let out a yelp of pain as it connected with his arm. He had blocked her blow, and she knew she had to get out of there before he could harm her. She pulled the aluminum bat back to take another swing and then she planned to run, but he pulled the bat from her hands. The blow that struck her cheek sent her flying back and into a rack of bras. She landed with a thud, and pain throbbed at her side as her ribs connected with the metal rack. She pulled her phone from her pocket and hit *call*.

"Don't think this is over, bitch. I'll be back for you," the intruder snarled in a low voice, and then he disappeared.

Debbie tried to get up, but her limbs began to shake. The sound of a voice calling from her phone sent relief coursing through her. She placed the phone to her ear and spoke.

Minutes later there were flashing lights outside her shop window. Debbie was still shaking and too weak to stand. She crawled to the shop door and unlocked it. The sight of the two sheriffs striding into her store made her feel safe for the first time since she'd heard the noise in her shop. She had met the two sheriffs when she had first come to town and was now very thankful she had. Sheriff Luke Sun-Walker helped her to her feet and then picked her up into his arms. He strode over to her counter and placed her on the stool. Sheriff Damon Osborne found the light switches and turned them on.

"Damon, get some ice from the kitchen," Luke ordered after checking to see if Debbie was all right. "He hit you, didn't he? You have a red cheek and your face is already swelling," Luke stated.

Debbie thanked Damon for the ice wrapped in a towel and winced as she placed it to her face. Luke began to ask questions. She was in the midst of giving Luke her statement when the squeal of tires screeching to a stop outside drew her attention. The sight of Daniel and Britt striding through her shop door made her pussy leak her juices. They pinned her with their eyes as they walked toward her.

"Are you all right, baby? Are you hurt? Let me see," Britt said and pulled the towel from her face. He winced when he saw her cheek, and she flinched back as his eyes filled with fury. "Easy, Deb. I'm not going to hurt you. Daniel, go help Damon and see how the bastard got in. Are you hurt anywhere else?"

"No. I'm fine. Stop fussing," Debbie replied in a wobbly voice. She sucked in a breath and tried to get her emotions under control. She turned to Luke and finished giving her statement. This time when she looked at Britt and saw his anger, she knew it was directed at her.

"Why the hell didn't you just call 9-1-1? Why did you come down here at all? You could have been killed. Your shop is not as important as your life, Debbie. You are not to ever risk yourself like that again."

"I beg your pardon? How dare you speak to me like that! I can't believe you. Please, just leave."

"I'm not going anywhere, baby. You belong to me and Daniel. If you won't take care of yourself then we'll have to do it for you. You go on upstairs and pack a bag. You're not staying here by yourself. You're coming home with us."

Debbie was glad that Luke had moved away and was now conversing with Damon and Daniel. She would have felt humiliated if they had heard what Britt was saying to her.

"No. I don't belong to anyone and I'm not going with you."

"Okay, I'll stay here with you. I'm not leaving you alone. I heard what you told Luke. Do you honestly think I am going to leave you unprotected when that bastard said he was going to come back for you?"

"You can't stay here. There's no room," Debbie said through clenched teeth. She was desperate to get rid of him. She was only holding on to the control of her emotions by a thread. She shivered again and couldn't seem to stop. She had never felt so cold in her life.

"You have two options, baby. Either you come home with us or we stay here," Britt stated in a steely voice.

There was no way she was letting one of them stay with her, let alone both, but she really didn't want to be alone. She felt violated and didn't think she would never feel secure in her apartment and shop again. She gave a sigh of resignation and stood up on wobbly legs. She felt a slight burn in her side and placed her hands over her ribs. She would have been all right if Britt hadn't reached out to steady her. His touch was enough to break through the tight control she had placed on her emotions. The first sob to erupt from her throat surprised even her. She buried her head against Britt's muscular chest and cried.

He picked her up in his arms, and then he was moving. He carried her up to her apartment and sank down onto the small sofa in her living room. He cradled her against him and rocked her comfortingly until the storm had passed.

Debbie felt like a fool for falling apart in front of him. She tried to push up and get off his lap, but he only tightened his hold. "Please, let me up." She was surprised when he complied, and she scrambled to her feet.

"Let me see your side," Britt demanded as he rose to his feet.

"That's not necessary. I'm fine."

"That wasn't a question," Britt replied gently as he took her chin in his hand. "I saw you holding your side and grimace in pain. Let me see."

"I don't think—"

"Debbie, I'm not letting you go anywhere until you show me."

Debbie sighed with resignation and pulled her sweater up at the side, being careful not to expose her braless breast.

"Son of a bitch. You already have a bruise and your skin is scraped. How did this happen?"

"When he hit me I fell into a rack."

"Have you got a first-aid kit?"

"Yes, but it's not necessary. It's only a scrape."

"It is necessary. You were scraped by metal. When was your last tetanus shot?"

"A couple of years ago. I'm fine, Britt."

"So you keep saying. Where is the kit?"

"In the bathroom."

Debbie wasn't prepared to be swept off her feet again. She shrieked and then clung to Britt's shoulders as he carried her into the bathroom. She cringed a little when Britt began to clean the scrape because it stung, but she kept quiet. She turned her head toward the footsteps she heard, and then Daniel stood in the doorway.

"Is she okay? I heard her cry out."

"She's fine," Britt replied as he finished tending her.

"She is right here, thank you very much," Debbie snapped.

"I know that, honey," Daniel said with a smirk in her direction.

"Come on. I'll help you pack a bag," Britt stated.

"I haven't said I'm coming with you," Debbie spat out.

"Okay. It looks like we're staying here. It might be a little cramped with all of us in your bed, but hey, I can handle it."

"What? No. You are not staying here or getting in my bed."

"I've already told you your choices, baby. If you won't come home with us then we're staying here. I'm not leaving you in harm's way. So you'd better make up your mind. What's it going to be?" Britt asked.

Debbie didn't answer. She stormed out of the bathroom, pushing her way past Daniel, and pulled her bag from her closet. She was too mad to take any notice of what she threw into the bag. The sight of a smiling Daniel lounging against the wall didn't improve her mood. She scowled at him and ignored him as she pulled out some underwear and hurled it toward her bag. She stormed past him and collected her toiletries and shoved them in her bag, too. As soon as the bag was zipped up, he took it from her. She flinched when Daniel's hand brushed hers.

"Do you have everything you want?" Daniel asked.

Debbie had no idea, but she wasn't about to tell him. So she just gave a nod.

"Okay, come on, honey. Let's get you home and settled in," Daniel stated.

Debbie didn't like the way those words sounded. They sounded too intimate to her, and she felt as if her life would never be the same again from that moment on. She pushed her thoughts aside and berated herself for being fanciful. She was only staying in their house one night, and first thing Monday morning she was going to the local security company and buying the best security system and locks money could buy. She knew she should have done that from the first, but lack of money hadn't allowed for such a luxury. She didn't care what it cost her now. She just wanted to feel safe in her own shop and apartment again.

Chapter Five

Debbie sighed as Britt slowed his truck and turned onto a drive. She looked around at the landscaped gardens as the headlights swept over them. From what she could see, someone had paid a lot of attention to the garden. The house was illuminated in the light, and she gasped as she got the first look of their home. It was breathtaking. It reminded her of a Victorian cottage she had once seen in a magazine, but on a much larger scale. The house had white boards with blue trim and lace ironwork bordering a wraparound veranda. Britt brought the truck to a stop and pushed a button on his dashboard. The doors to the four-car garage slid open automatically and silently. While Britt unlocked the door into the house, Daniel came around to Debbie's side of the car.

"Are you all right, honey?" Daniel asked when he opened her door for her.

"Yes, I'm fine. Thank you," Debbie said when he took her hand to help her from the truck.

"Let's get you inside and settled," Daniel said and took her bag from her, guiding her with a hand to her lower back.

Debbie couldn't contain her shiver at the contact. Even though she had a sweater separating their skin, she could feel the heat of him through the material.

She looked around curiously as he directed her down the hallway. He reached around her and opened the door to a bedroom. The room was bigger than her whole apartment. The ceiling was white, and three walls were painted a light-cream color. The wall behind the massive bed was a light mauve and set the room off perfectly.

"Oh my. This room is gorgeous. That bed is big enough for four people," Debbie stated.

"There's a bathroom through that door and a robe is over there. Why don't you get settled? Do you want a drink?" Daniel asked.

"Yes, please. A cup of tea would be nice if you have it."

"Sure. It'll be ready when you come out," Daniel said. He surprised her by pulling her into his arms and giving her a hug, and he kissed her on her temple. "Take your time, honey."

Debbie watched him disappear out the door. She sank down onto the side of the bed and wondered what the hell she had gotten herself into. She had tried to refuse their attentions, but she knew she was in trouble. Daniel and Britt wanted to get her into bed, and she was going to let them. She was tired of trying to keep them at arm's length. She wanted to feel their hands and mouths on her body. She wanted to have the freedom to kiss and touch them whenever she liked.

So she would have a fling with them. She would keep her heart locked away tight. The last thing she wanted to do was fall in love with them and then have them hurt her. She'd been there and done that, and she wasn't about to do it again. She knew eventually things would go sour. They always did when she was involved in a relationship.

But the thought of giving her body to them and then having them leave her pierced her heart with pain. She already had feelings for the two Delaney brothers. She wondered if she was getting in over her head. Could she really give them her body and not involve her heart? When all was said and done, she just wasn't strong enough to resist them.

Debbie followed the sound of their deep, rumbling voices and found the kitchen. It was a chef's dream. All the appliances were state-of-the-art stainless steel. The counters were a black-flecked stone, and the cupboards were a high-gloss white. The backsplash was also all stainless steel. There were black-leather stools near the bench, and the dining room was attached but even bigger than the kitchen. She could just imagine cooking up a storm in this kitchen and serving guests dinner around the long table.

"Your kitchen is a dream. You have a beautiful home," Debbie said as she walked over to the table and sat. "Thank you for my tea."

"You're welcome, honey."

"Do either of you ever use that kitchen?"

"Sure we do, baby. We can cook. We had to learn to be self-sufficient. We couldn't stand having to live on takeout all the time," Britt replied.

"Well, at least it's not going to waste."

"You're still a little pale. Are you feeling okay, honey?" Daniel asked.

"Yes, I'm fine. Just tired I guess. It's been a long night."

"That it has. Why don't you go and crawl into bed? You're exhausted," Britt avowed.

"Yes, I will," Deb replied and rose to her feet. She picked up her mug and rinsed it, leaving it in the sink. "Well, thank you for coming to help me. Good night."

"Sleep well, honey," Daniel called.

"Night, baby," Britt said.

Debbie walked down the hall to her temporary room and closed the door with a sigh. She stripped off her clothes and rummaged in her bag for a nightgown. She sighed with frustration when she realized she hadn't packed one. Instead she had packed two camisoles. As she slipped one over her head, she smiled at the coincidence when she realized it matched the mauve on the wall. She slipped into bed and turned off the bedside lamp and was asleep moments later.

* * * *

"Shit, Britt. I've never been so scared in my life. I thought for sure when the call came through Glen Parker had gotten to her," Daniel said and ran hand down his face in frustration.

"Yeah me, too, but burglary's not his usual MO. I can't believe she confronted the burglar. The fact she got hurt tears me to the bone. We're going to have to try and get her to move in here with us. I don't want her living alone anymore. That bastard could come back for her anytime. Did Luke find any prints on the lock or cash register?"

"No. He had to be wearing gloves. Deb said she thought he was wearing a balaclava too, so she didn't see his face. All she told Luke was that the bastard was big. God, I want to protect her from the world and never let her leave the house again," Daniel said with a sigh.

"Yeah like that's going to happen. She hates being told what to do. She's too wary of men since her ex hurt Leah, to let her guard down," Britt stated.

"When she looks at you I can see sadness in her eyes. She looks so lonely and vulnerable, but when you look at her she tries to be so calm and cool. God, I want to take her in my arms and just hold her. I want to take that loneliness away."

"She looks at you the same way," Britt said. "I want her to open up with us. I want to know everything about her. I want to know her hopes and dreams and make them come true. I want to know about her family and what her favorite foods are, and I want her to drop those walls she's enclosed her heart in."

"Well, at least we know what her favorite color is. You should have seen her face when she walked into her room. Her eyes lit up and her whole face was filled with joy when she saw her room for the first time. She looked so gorgeous. My cock is so hard and I swear my balls are turning blue. I love the fact she wears lavender, she smells so good I just want to take a bite out of her," Daniel said on a groan. "Shit, now I'm going to have to jack off just so I can get to sleep."

"Me, too. Do you think she knows we decorated that room for her?" Britt asked.

"No. She has no idea, thank God. If she did she would have been out the door in a shot. I'm going to bed to get a couple of hours' sleep. I have a feeling tomorrow's going to be a long day."

"Yeah, I hear ya. She's going to insist we take her home again," Britt predicted.

"Yeah, but you and I know that's not going to happen," Daniel said with a smirk. "G'night"

"Night."

Daniel had just settled into bed when he heard the first scream. He was up in a flash, had his gun in his hand, and was in Debbie's room before he took his next breath. He scanned the interior and hid his gun in the waistband of his boxers when he realized Debbie was dreaming. He flicked on the bedside lamp and reached for her. He cradled her against his bare chest and tried to wake her gently.

"What's wrong?" Britt asked as he entered the room. His brother's hair was still damp from his shower.

"Nightmare," he answered. "Wake up, honey. Come on, you're safe here."

Daniel was glad he had such lightning-fast reflexes as he ducked her flying fist. He gently took her hand in his and held on to it so Debbie couldn't hurt herself. Britt sat down beside him and Deb. His brother took her free hand in his and began to gently rub her back. Slowly, the tension in her body released and she stopped trying to fight him and Britt. She slumped against his chest, and he felt her tears trickling down his bare skin.

"I'm sorry," she whispered.

"You have nothing to be sorry for, honey. Take a few deep breaths and relax, Deb. You're safe here with us. We won't ever hurt you. I promise. Are you okay now?" Daniel asked.

"Yeah."

"Good," Daniel replied and lifted her back onto the bed. He covered her up and sighed with relief that her body was now nearly completely out of sight. His balls ached, and his cock was fully erect. He didn't want her to see how hard he was, so he reached over and turned off the bedside lamp and then stood.

"Don't." Her quiet whisper reached his ears.

"Don't what, honey?"

"Please don't leave me. I don't want to be alone."

Daniel knew she had no idea what she was asking of them, but he couldn't leave her when she was so scared. He sighed and prayed he would be able to keep his libido under control. He slid the gun out of his shorts and placed it on the bedside table.

"Scoot into the middle, honey," Daniel said then climbed into bed. She snuggled up onto his chest once he was settled in the bed on his back. He wrapped an arm around her and pulled her in closer. He felt the mattress move as Britt climbed in as well. She sighed, and Britt cuddled up to her back. His brother accidentally brushed his side with his hand.

"You're safe, baby. Close your eyes and go to sleep," Britt said.

Daniel knew the moment Debbie had drifted off to sleep again. The last of the tension in her body was gone, and her breathing deepened. He knew he wouldn't be able to sleep a wink with her body plastered along his. He sighed and tried to relax but only tensed even more when she threw a leg over his hips, her thigh resting on his throbbing dick. He was just glad it was only a couple of hours until dawn. He didn't know how long he could stand the torture of lying beside her without being able to love her. It was going to be the longest couple of hours he had ever endured. He knew his brother was suffering just as he was when he groaned as Debbie wiggled in her sleep. On the other hand, as excruciating as this was, she was exactly where they wanted her for the first time. He just hoped they could convince her to stay.

He and Britt had met Debbie nearly six months ago, after they moved to Slick Rock from Phoenix, Arizona. He had known in that instant she was the woman they had been waiting for. Before they began courting her, he and Britt had often slipped questions about Debbie into conversations with Seamus and Connell O'Hara. Leah, too, had told them quite a bit about Debbie Newsome, but not enough to satisfy his curiosity. He wanted to know so much more, and he knew Britt did as well.

They were going to have to be careful with her and not push her too hard or too fast. He didn't want to give her any reasons to run from them when her history already made her skittish. He would never do or say anything to make her feel uncomfortable about her past. He and his brother had had countless women over the years, and he wouldn't feel right if she asked him about the previous women in his life.

Those days were over, though. Even if it was way too soon to go declaring his feelings for her, he was in love with her already. This room was hers as far as he and Britt were concerned, and he couldn't wait to have her living here permanently.

Chapter Six

Debbie stared at the expanse of tanned muscular chests on display. Her clit throbbed and she gulped in reaction as she devoured Britt and Daniel with her eyes.

Debbie managed to lift her gaze from them and looked at the clock on the dining-room wall. She gasped when she saw the time. It was 10:00 a.m., and she couldn't believe she had slept so late. Of course she knew why she had, but she still felt guilty. She had never been one of those people who could sleep to all hours.

She hesitated in the doorway. Neither of the men had bothered to put shirts on. She gulped at the sight of their naked skin. They were both sipping coffee and chatting, unaware of her presence. She was about to duck back around the corner and hide in her room, but her movement must have alerted Britt to her presence. He looked up and pinned her with his blue eyes.

"Hey, baby, come on in. Do you want coffee?"

Debbie didn't think she would be able to answer without her voice squeaking, so she just gave a slight nod. She couldn't help but stare at Britt's broad chest, muscles moving and striating beneath his skin as he grabbed a mug from the cupboard and poured her some of the dark brew out of the pot. He walked toward her, slid his large, warm hand down her arm, and took her hand in his. He led her over to the table, placed the mug down, and pulled a chair out for her. When she was seated she wrapped her hands around the mug and looked into the coffee. She didn't want to be caught ogling him and Daniel and she knew she wouldn't be able to keep her eyes from wandering over their naked chests, so she kept her eyes lowered.

"How are you feeling, honey?" Daniel asked from beside her. She speculated on whether Britt had purposely placed her in the empty seat between him and Daniel.

"Fine, thanks," she replied and cursed the sound of her own breathless voice.

"Are you sure, Debbie? You're looking a little flushed," Britt said, and then placed his palm on her forehead. Debbie jerked back from the unexpected touch and then felt her cheeks heat, embarrassed about overreacting.

"Look at me, baby," Britt requested gently.

Debbie lowered her eyelashes even more and shook her head, refusing to meet his eyes.

"What's wrong, baby? Have we done something to hurt you?"

Again she just shook her head. She felt Britt's thumb and finger on her chin, and he lifted her face up to his.

"Do we make you uncomfortable, Deb?"

Debbie opened her mouth to deny it, but then changed her mind. "Yes."

"Why?"

"You don't have any shirts on," she replied.

"Why does that unnerve you, baby?" Britt asked. "I'm sure you've seen lots of men without their shirts on."

"Because I can't keep my eyes off you," Debbie muttered truthfully. She felt her cheeks heat even more when a slow smile spread across Britt's face. He let go of her chin and took her hand in his. He gently pulled her from her chair and onto his lap.

"I don't mind that you want to look at me, baby. You can touch me if you want," Britt rumbled.

Debbie lowered her head, using her unbound hair to hide her heated cheeks. She yearned to touch him and Daniel so much, but she knew if she did it wouldn't stop there. She squirmed slightly on his lap, trying to ease the throb in her clit. She felt her liquid arousal seep from her pussy to dampen her panties. She froze when she felt the bulge under her ass and didn't want to move in case she aroused Britt further. She felt one of his large, muscular arms wrap around her waist, and then he tilted back gently so that her head resting on his shoulder.

She looked up when he brushed the hair back from her face and stared at her. Her pussy clenched at the heat she saw in his eyes, and she was lost, drowning in the depths of the blue pools.

"You have no idea how beautiful you are, do you?" Britt said. She shook her head minimally as he lowered his head toward her. She sighed at the first contact of his lips. She had waited for this ever since the night of the cookout at Leah's.

She moaned when his tongue licked over her flesh and opened up to him. His tongue swept into her mouth, and she drowned in liquid desire. Her womb felt heavy, and her body temperature shot up as she slid her tongue along his. He tasted so good. She knew she would never be able to get enough. His shoulder moved, and his fingers stroked along her neck as his mouth devoured hers. It was a kiss that would forever be embedded in her mind. It was so carnal, but also soft, gentle, and loving. She whimpered in protest as he removed his mouth from hers and stared down at her. The fire in his eyes was nearly enough to frighten her, but it also made her crave more of him.

Debbie turned her head when she felt Daniel's touch. She saw the same intensity in his green eyes she had seen in Britt's. He reached down and plucked her off Britt's lap and held her against him. She wrapped her arms around his neck and her legs around his waist. She closed her eyes when he leaned down and kissed her. Her body was tense with need but also boneless with desire. She clung to him as their lips met and opened up to let him ravish her mouth.

Even though they were brothers their kisses were totally different. It surprised her that Britt's kisses were gentler than Daniel's. He coaxed and asked for a response, where Daniel demanded one. To her it was a contradiction to their personalities, but no less arousing.

She mewled in the back of her throat when Daniel sucked her tongue into his mouth. When he released her muscle, he nipped at her bottom lip. She couldn't get close enough to him and tried to bury herself against his body. Her hips moved, and she moaned when she felt his hard cock come in contact with her aching clit, beneath her clothes.

"I want you so damn much, honey. Will you let me make you feel good?" Daniel asked, his voice raspy from his arousal.

Debbie hesitated to answer. She wanted, needed them both to touch her, but she knew as soon as she gave them permission, things would change between them irrevocably. They would never be able to turn back the clock. She whimpered when Daniel thrust his hips into hers. The contact of his cock to her pussy made her cunt gush more cream. She was on fire, and she knew only Daniel and Britt could quench it. She was thankful Daniel didn't try to sway her decision in any way and finally closed her eyes and nodded her head.

"Open your eyes and look at me, honey," Daniel said quietly. When she did what he asked, he held her gaze with his and carried her to the kitchen counter. He placed her butt on the stone bench top, and then his fingers were at the waistband of her jeans. Her button popped open, and then he lowered the zipper. She looked up to see Britt moving over to them and knew this was what she wanted. This was what she had been waiting for.

"Lift up, baby," Britt said. His hands steadied her waist, and she held on to his large biceps while Daniel pulled her jeans and panties down her legs and off. She gasped as the cold of the stone bench made contact with her naked skin.

"God, you smell good, honey. I can smell your cream from here. Open up for me, Deb," Daniel rasped as he gently separated her thighs. "I need to taste you, honey."

"Fuck. Your bare pussy is gorgeous, baby. Lift your arms and let me get your shirt off," Britt said. She lifted her arms as he took the hem of her T-shirt in his big hands and pulled it over her head. "God, I love what you wear beneath your clothes, Deb. You're so sexy."

Debbie whimpered as Daniel wrapped his arms around her thighs and held her legs wide. He lowered his head and flicked his tongue over her clit. She leaned back on her arms and closed her eyes. She felt Britt flip open her bra clasp, and her breasts spilled free. Daniel wrenched a cry from her when he slid his tongue down through her folds and caressed her pussy. Britt's lips closed around one of her hard nipples. She mewled as he began to suckle on her breast. She was so hot for them she was close to climax already. Her cunt clenched as heat traveled from her breasts down her belly, into her womb, and pooled in her vagina.

"You taste so good, honey. I want you to come for me. I want to taste more of that sweet cream of yours," Daniel rasped in a deep voice.

Debbie sobbed when Daniel slid a finger into her pussy, easing his way in until he could go no farther. He laved his tongue over the sensitive, engorged bundle of nerves at the top of her slit and lapped her clit, over and over again. He began to pump his digit in and out of her sheath, and Debbie let her head drop back as waves of pleasure rolled over her. She cried out when Daniel added another finger to her pussy and glided them in and out, creating a pleasurable friction against her inner walls. Tingles traveled up and down her body and gooseflesh rose up all over her naked skin.

She felt Britt's hand in her hair, and he lifted her mouth to his and kissed her with openmouthed carnality. Her limbs began to shake, and she was on the verge of climax. The muscles of her pussy gathered into a tight coil, and with one more sweep of his tongue over her clit, Daniel sent her careening out into space. She screamed into Britt's mouth as stars formed before her eyes, and Daniel kept thrusting his fingers in and out of her pussy, enhancing her pleasure until the last wave finally died away.

Britt took his mouth from hers and rubbed a soothing hand over her belly. Daniel lifted his head from between her splayed thighs and caressed her legs. She had never felt such an explosive climax before. She knew then and there she was in danger of losing her heart to the two men who had just given her so much pleasure. Daniel stood up, and she couldn't help but see the huge bulge in his jeans. She looked over to Britt and saw his cock was hard, too. Her pussy clenched, and she couldn't believe just one glance at their crotches had her embers flaring again. She wanted to reach out and rub her hands up along the lengths of their shafts but was too shy to make that move. She didn't know what to say or how to react now that they had touched her.

"You are the sexiest woman I have ever met," Daniel said as he looked into her eyes.

Britt cupped her cheek with his palm and turned her head toward him. "Baby, will you let us love you? We want to make love with you, together."

Debbie knew she had gone too far to back out now. She knew if she said no, they wouldn't push her, but she wasn't going to say no. She wanted this more than her next breath of air.

"Yes," Debbie said, and then she was in Britt's arms as he carried her naked through the house to her bedroom.

Chapter Seven

"You are so fucking sexy, Deb. I want you so much I ache with it," Britt stated in a deep, gravelly voice.

Britt heard Debbie sigh as he lowered her to the bed. His brother lay down beside their woman and took her mouth beneath his own. Britt shucked his jeans and boxers and crawled onto the bed from the foot. He slid his hands up her smooth shins and then over the silky skin of her inner thighs as he parted her legs. He wanted to taste her so badly. He had nearly come in his pants when Daniel made her orgasm. She looked so sexy when she was in the throes of climax. He wanted to pleasure her over and over again until she couldn't take any more, but he was too needy to do that today.

He bent over and licked her from anus to clit and back again. His cock jerked at the sounds she made as he and his brother pleasured their woman. He settled down onto the bed and devoured her pussy with his lips and tongue. He slid two fingers into her cunt and began to thrust them in and out of her sheath. She bucked her hips up, and he knew she liked what he was doing to her. He didn't want her going over this time, but he was going to bring her right to the edge. He sucked her clit into his mouth and flicked it with his tongue. When he felt her pussy walls quiver around his pumping fingers, he knew she was close to release.

Britt sat up between her thighs, sheathed his cock with a condom he had placed on the mattress, and then he began to push into her body. He groaned as her delicate pink flesh separated and gave way to his gentle intrusion. He held still as she rippled around the head of his cock and waited for a signal from her to continue. She looked so sexy with her neck arched, her eyes closed, and his brother sucking on one nipple and pinching on the other. She wriggled her hips, and he knew she was trying to get more of him inside her.

He clasped her hips and began to forge his way into her tight, wet cunt. He stopped when he was halfway inside. He rubbed his thumb over the smooth, warm skin of her hip and used the fingers of his other hand to lightly massage her clit. She was so tight that he was having trouble penetrating her. She began to open up and relax around him, so he slid slowly and gently all the way into her until his balls were touching her ass. He knew he was a big man and was surprised when she took all of him. He'd never had that happen before. She fit him like a glove, and he knew they had been made for each other.

Britt slid back and then pushed in again. He wanted to speed up and pound in and out of her until they both reached climax, but he wasn't willing to do that in case he hurt her. Daniel moved to her side, and Britt picked her up in his arms until she straddled his hips. He held her still while he scooted to the middle of the bed, and then he lay down on his back. He held her hip with one hand and slid the other up to cup her breast and fondle her nipple. Glazed with passion, her stormy gray eyes looked down at him from beneath heavy eyelids. Her lips were full and red from their kisses, and he could just imagine what that mouth would feel like wrapped around his dick.

He tugged her down to him until she laid on his chest, her hard nipples brushing his skin, and wrapped an arm around her waist as he cupped the back of her head with his free hand. He connected his mouth to hers and swept his tongue into her moist cavern. Her enthusiastic response pulled a groan from deep in his chest. He knew what his brother was about to do, and he wanted to keep her distracted so she wouldn't tense up again.

Britt felt her flinch and knew Daniel was rubbing lube into her ass. She pulled her mouth from his and gulped air into her lungs. He felt her tense, and she pulled into a half-sitting position. Even though he knew it had been inevitable that she would tighten up, he kept trying to distract her. He clasped her nipples between his finger and thumb, squeezing them hard enough to give her a bite of pain, yet not hard enough to hurt her.

"Easy, honey. Just breathe and relax for me. That's it. Good girl," Daniel crooned.

Britt felt Debbie's pussy tighten and knew his brother was stretching her ass with his fingers. His cock jerked as her muscles clenched on his erection. He had to breathe with Deb so he could try and control his own desire. He wanted so badly to pump his hips in and out of her, hard and fast, until they both found release. And then he wanted to do it over and over again. She felt like hot liquid silk around his dick, and he never wanted to leave her body.

"I'm coming in now, Deb. Try and keep those muscles loose for me," Daniel panted.

Britt heard Deb moan, and he released her nipples as she slumped down on him. He felt her lift her hips slightly so his brother would have better access to her anus. She was such a responsive little thing. Her breath was sobbing out, and she was trying to wriggle on his cock. He clasped the globes of her butt and held her still while Daniel worked his way slowly into her body. She was so tight with two cocks now embedded in her, and he was in danger of losing control.

He looked over her head and Daniel gave him a nod, and then they both helped her to sit up between them. She mewled, and he groaned as his cock slid into her a little deeper. He could feel the head of his dick touching her cervix. He felt Daniel slide out of her ass and hold still for a moment, and then his brother pushed back in.

Britt pulled back until his hard flesh was resting just inside her pussy, and then he pushed all the way in again. He and Daniel set up a slow, easy pace of glide in and retreat, sliding their hard dicks in and out of both of her holes. He had never felt anything so exquisite. He knew in that moment that all the women before her were inconsequential. There were no words to describe the feeling of making love to the woman who had stolen his heart. It was just too special to even begin to try to describe.

He and Daniel thrust their hips alternately, making sure one of them was buried in her body as the other withdrew. Britt wanted to pick up the pace, but he didn't want the pleasure he was giving and receiving to end too soon. The sounds their woman made as they loved her made his breath catch. The sight of her aroused and being pleasured pierced his heart. He would do everything he could to make sure she was happy, content, and safe.

Britt pushed his hips up and felt his balls churning with the need for release. He looked at his brother and gave him a nod. Letting him know silently it was time to up the ante and make their woman climax before he did. He pulled out and thrust back into her a bit faster and harder than the previous times. His brother kept pace with him. They increased their rhythm of thrust and retreat until Debbie was keening in the back of her throat. Faster and faster his and Daniel's flesh slapped into hers.

* * * *

Debbie couldn't get enough of them. She'd had sex before, but she had never felt so much pleasure and such a connection to the two men loving her. She wanted them to love on her hard and fast, but they kept the pace slow and easy. She didn't know how long they had been sliding in and out of her ass and pussy, but she didn't want the pleasure to stop, ever. The sensation of having two cocks in her body made her feel so erotically feminine and oh, so full. Their cocks were huge, and at first she had been frightened they would hurt her as Britt, then Daniel eased their way into her body.

The friction of their cocks gliding along the walls of her sheath and canal was nearly too much pleasure to bear. She wanted them, no, needed them to move faster and harder. She could feel the tension building up in her muscles as liquid lava traveled through her blood and pooled in her womb and pussy. She clung to Britt's massive biceps as she half sat up over him, and then she cried out as he pinched both her nipples between finger and thumb. She threw her head back and keened as the decadence of their lovemaking consumed her. She knew she was getting close to the edge and wanted to race to the inevitable pinnacle.

She cried out as Britt and Daniel slowly picked up the pace of their thrusting cocks, pumping in and retreating, forging into her body a bit faster, harder, and deeper with every forward movement. She could feel the walls of her own pussy and ass rippling around the two cocks as they accelerated, the sound of their harsh breathing permeating the air as they made love to her. Her body began to tighten as the pleasure grew, and she melted, prone, in a pool of desire. Slumping onto Britt, she lifted her hips slightly to give Daniel better access to her back entrance. They must have taken that as a sign she was getting close to orgasm, because they released their tight control and began to pound in and out of her holes.

She tried to fight the feelings running through her. She was frightened by the intensity and didn't know if she could handle the fall. Her limbs and belly trembled. Her whole body shook, and she didn't want to orgasm. The sensations were too big, too much for her to comprehend and handle. She didn't want it to end yet and was too afraid to let go. Her heart was so full it was near to bursting and she didn't know how to handle it.

"Stop fighting it, honey," Daniel whispered in her ear.

"Let go, baby. We'll catch you," Britt stated breathlessly.

Debbie wiggled around between them, trying to take some of the powerful feelings away. They wouldn't let her. Daniel reached around her beneath her breasts and pulled her up into a sitting position. As she leaned back against his chest, he kneaded her breasts in his large hands.

Britt held her hip in one hand and slid his other down to the top of her slit. It was too much. She arched her neck, her head connecting with Daniel's shoulder, and screamed as Britt massaged her clit with a finger and Daniel pinched her nipples. Her body gathered in tightly, and then the spring snapped. They fucked her as she climaxed, never once stopping the shuttle of their cocks moving in and out of her body. Her pelvic-floor muscles contracted and released again and again and again. She felt her cream cover Britt's cock. Her body shook and trembled as she reached nirvana.

Debbie had never felt such bliss before and was scared she would crave these two men for the rest of her life. Daniel's breath hitched, and then he groaned as he spewed his seed into the condom. Britt began to roar and she looked down to watch his face contort with pleasure. His jaw was tight as he gritted his teeth and thrust up into her one more time. He gripped her hips in both hands and held still. His cock jerked inside her and his fluids filled the prophylactic.

Debbie had never seen anything so erotic in her whole life. She slumped down onto Britt, her body still giving the occasional quake as her lax muscles wouldn't hold her up anymore. The only sound in the room was their now-slowing breath, and she closed her eyes when she felt tears prick behind her eyeballs.

She didn't want them to see how much they had moved her emotionally as they made love to her. She knew if they saw her tears they would be worried they hurt her, and that was the last thing she wanted. She felt so vulnerable. With such ease, they had systematically torn down the walls she had built up around her heart. She had known from the beginning she should have kept these two men at arm's length. She already had strong feelings for them and didn't want to.

She didn't want to be ashamed and vulnerable again. As little as she wanted to hurt them, she was afraid that she would end up heartbroken. The only way around the situation was to go back to that cool, calm, collected persona she'd portrayed to them before. She wanted to shower, dress, and leave, but she didn't have her car and she knew Britt and Daniel were going to argue with her.

Debbie couldn't prevent her whimpering as Daniel withdrew his semierect cock from her ass and rose from the bed. She heard him in the bathroom, water running in the background. Britt rolled with her to the side, and his cock slipped from her pussy.

"Are you okay, baby?" Britt asked.

"Yeah, never better," Debbie replied. He must have heard something in her voice because he grabbed a handful of her hair and gently tilted her head up so he could see her face. His eyes narrowed as he looked at her.

"What's wrong, Deb?"

"Nothing."

"You're lying. I can hear it in your voice."

"I don't know what you're talking about," Debbie replied and pulled away from him. She stood and gave him a cool look before she spoke again. "I'm going to take a shower. When I'm done I want one of you to take me home."

Debbie entered the bathroom, completely ignoring Daniel as he stared at her. She turned on the shower, washed, then got out and dried off. By the time she had finished and entered the bedroom Daniel and Britt had left the room. She sighed with relief and dressed then packed her bag. She was going to have a fight on her hands, but she was going to get what she wanted in the end.

Chapter Eight

"What the hell is going on?" Daniel demanded as he entered the kitchen to see Britt pouring coffee.

"I don't know."

"Did you say or do something to upset her?" he asked, running his fingers through his hair in frustration.

"No. I didn't say a damn thing. When you left the room, I rolled her onto her side and looked at her. She had that cool mask on her face again. What the fuck, Daniel? I thought we were getting somewhere with her. She just accepted us into her bed and body and now she's turning away again. I'm not letting her leave. She could be in danger and I don't want her alone," Britt spat.

"You can't keep her here if she doesn't want to stay. We have to find out what the hell is wrong though. I don't like the pain I can see in her eyes."

"And how the fuck are we supposed to do that? She's clamming up again."

"Shit. I don't know. I just don't know," Daniel replied, then signaled his brother to keep quiet when he heard Deb coming toward them, her bag in her hand. She wanted to leave right then, but he wanted answers first. "What's going on, Debbie?"

"Nothing. I just have too much to do to idle the day away in bed. I do have a business to run, you know."

Daniel hated the way she was withdrawing from them. Her face was expressionless, a blank mask without any feeling, but her eyes told a different story. He knew she had a business which needed her attention. He also knew she was using it as an excuse to leave. He didn't want her to go, but he knew he couldn't force her to stay. He sighed with resignation and pulled his keys from his jeans pocket.

"Okay, then let's go. Are you sure this is what you want?" Daniel asked quietly. She didn't speak to him, just gave a nod of her head. He sighed again and headed out. He was at the truck before he realized he hadn't taken her bag from her. She had him so rattled he'd forgotten his manners. It was too late to take it from her now. She'd already opened the back door to put her bag in.

He was about to lift her into the passenger seat when there was a loud crash inside. The sound of something breaking and the roar of fury coming from his brother echoed his own sentiments. He saw Debbie flinch and bite her lip. He knew she felt responsible, but he also knew she wasn't about to change her mind. She slid into the seat, put her safety belt on, and clenched her hands in her lap.

She didn't talk to him at all on the trip back to her shop. He pulled the truck into the alley behind her store, and she didn't look at him when she gave him her thanks and climbed the stairs to her apartment. She never once looked back. She disappeared behind the closed door.

Daniel slammed his palm onto the steering wheel, savoring the pain, trying to get rid of the ache in his heart. It didn't help. He put the truck in gear and roared away. He and Britt couldn't look out for her personally now, but that didn't mean they couldn't make her as safe as possible. He pulled his cell from his pocket and called the after-hours number of the local security company. He didn't care how much it cost. By the end of today, Debbie's apartment and shop were going to have the best security system and locks money could buy.

As he pulled into the driveway, Britt was mowing the lawn. He had already used the edge trimmer, and he could tell by his brother's jerky movements he was still furious and in pain. He got out of the truck, went out back, and began to chop wood. By the time he and Britt were finished, they were both covered in sweat from their strenuous activities, and it hadn't helped one little bit.

Daniel was beside himself with worry for Debbie. He wanted to know what was going on inside that hard head of hers. There was only one person he could think of who might have an inkling as to what had gone wrong. He hurried inside and picked up the phone.

* * * *

The knock on the door to her apartment made her jump. Debbie didn't want to open the door in case it was Britt or Daniel, but she had never been a coward before. She wrenched the door open and was surprised to see the man from the local security company standing on the landing.

"Ms. Newsome, do you remember me? I'm Giles Alcott. My brothers Remy and Brandon helped you with your security system."

"Yes, I remember you, Mr. Alcott. How can I help you?"

"I'm here to update your system."

"Pardon?"

"I said—"

"I know what you said, Mr. Alcott, but I don't understand. I was going to call you tomorrow to replace the system I have, but since I haven't done that yet, I'd like to know what you're doing here."

"Please, call me Giles. Your new system and locks have already been paid for. My brothers are just getting the stuff out of the truck. Would you be able to open up your shop so we can get to work?"

"Giles, who the hell…Oh my God. Britt and Daniel did this, didn't they? Shit. Sorry, okay, just give a minute to get my keys, and call me Debbie or Deb," she said. Giles headed down the steps as she turned back into her apartment, muttering to herself. She grabbed her keys and stormed downstairs and opened up. "Of all the arrogant assholes I've ever met, they take the cake. I can't believe they did this. God, why did they have to be so nice after I treated them like shit? I'll just have to pay them back every penny. Yes, that's what I'll do. They won't be able to hold this over my head then. Oh God. They would never do that. What am I thinking? I'm such a bitch. What is wrong with me?"

Debbie cut off her monologue and pursed her lips. Remy and Brandon smiled at her as they left her at the door and got to work. She was heading back up to her apartment when footsteps sounded behind her. Turning, she raised an eyebrow in query when she saw Giles following her up the stairs.

"The package includes an alarm and sensors for your apartment as well as new locks for your windows and doors," Giles stated.

"For God's sake," Debbie muttered and led the way inside. She excused herself when she heard her phone ringing.

"Hello."

"Hi there, Deb, I was wondering if you're free to share a bottle of wine and some snacks," Leah said.

"Um, where? I have Giles, Remy, and Brandon Alcott putting in a new security system here at the moment."

"Then I'll come there. I'll see you soon."

"Okay," Debbie replied then looked at the handset because Leah had already disconnected the call. She replaced the receiver and went to her kitchen to rummage in her fridge and cupboards. Ten minutes later, she heard Leah knock on the door. She let Leah in and led her into the small kitchenette where she had a small table and four chairs. She had figured it would be easier to talk in there since Giles was working in her living room and bedroom at the moment.

"So what's been going on?" Leah asked as Debbie got out the bottle opener.

"I was burgled last night."

"Oh my God. Are you okay? Sit down, I'll do that. Tell me what happened."

Debbie ran through the events of the previous night and how she ended up staying with Britt and Daniel. She left out the part about having sex with them and took a sip of her wine. She eyed Leah's glass of juice and cursed the fact she had again forgotten her friend wouldn't be drinking. She guessed she was just too rattled to think straight.

"Well, I'm glad you had the sense to upgrade your security. I know you'll probably sleep better with the new system and so will I. Are you sure you're all right to stay here by yourself?"

"Yes, thanks, Leah. I'll be fine. I didn't call the security company though, Britt and Daniel did. I was going to tomorrow, but they didn't give me a chance," Deb said and frowned.

"They obviously care for you and want to know you're safe. That is so romantic. So when are you going to take them to bed?"

Leah had asked Debbie the one question she was hoping she wouldn't. She felt her cheeks heat and lowered her head, trying to shield her face with her hair.

"Oh my. You already have, haven't you?" Leah asked. "So what was it like? I want all the deets, girl, and I'm not leaving until I get them."

To her and Leah's surprise, Debbie burst into tears. She didn't even really know why she was crying. No, that wasn't true. She was lying to herself. Leah stood up and held her while she cried. Once she had stopped and was in control again, she began to talk. And when she started she couldn't stop. All her insecurities poured out, and she even told Leah how much Britt and Daniel were working their way into her heart. Leah was the only person she could be totally honest with, and she valued her friendship greatly.

"Deb, you're being too hard on yourself. Connell and Seamus were flattered when you came to them. Of course I was jealous at first, but I quickly got over that once my men explained the situation to me. You were hurting when you were with them, and men being men, they didn't refuse when they should have. You had nothing to do with what your ex did to me. I know you have feelings for those two Delaney men. You think you can hide it from yourself, and you can keep believing that if you want to, but you and I both know you want them and are maybe a little in love with them.

"We all take risks when we put our hearts on the line, honey. Love is…can be a scary thing. But you don't know how things will pan out with them. Don't you want to try and have a relationship with them? You never know, they maybe just what you're looking for."

"I can't, Leah. I just can't open myself up to being hurt again. It's just too painful."

The sympathy in Leah's expression iced over, and she firmed her mouth. "And here I was thinking you were the bravest woman I know. I wouldn't have confronted a burglar, but you did. You could have been killed, for crying out loud. You have a bruise on your cheek and here you are telling me you're too scared to have a relationship that could be the best thing you ever had. You're a coward, Debbie Newsome. I love you like a sister, but right now I'm too mad with you to stay. I'll call you in a few days." Leah said. Debbie watched openmouthed as Leah gave her a quick hug then left.

Debbie was in turmoil. Distraught with what Leah had said, she downed the contents of her wine glass and poured another. She sat in her kitchen nibbling and drinking until her vision went hazy. She tried to concentrate when Giles came into the kitchen and explained how to use her newly installed security system. She gave him a wave when he smiled at her and left. The door closed quietly behind him, and she was alone once more.

Chapter Nine

Debbie felt like death warmed up, but she put on a smile and opened her shop to her first customers at nine the next morning. She was glad her alarm had been on because she knew she wouldn't have awoken by herself. She'd even put on some makeup this morning, trying to cover up her pallor. She had popped some painkillers with nearly a gallon of water before she had made her way to the store, and she knew it would be a while before they began to work. She sipped at her coffee as three women browsed the racks of lingerie, giggling and chatting as they did.

She looked up when the bell tinkled, admitting a tall man dressed in a suit. She had never seen him before, but that didn't mean he didn't live in Slick Rock. Even though it was a small town, she knew she would never meet all the residents.

Debbie felt her skin crawl as he stopped in front of the counter. She had no idea why, but he gave her the jitters. "Hello, can I help you?" she asked politely.

The man gave her a broad smile. "Yes, thanks. I'm looking for a gift for my girl and thought you could help me."

"Sure. Do you have anything particular in mind?"

"Not really. I thought you could suggest a couple of things."

"Okay. Well, come with me and I can point out a few items. Do you know her size?" Debbie asked as she looked up at him. She tried not to shudder when his eyes ran over her.

"I'd say she's about your size."

"All right. I think a teddy or a set of underpants and a camisole. Do you know what color she likes?"

"She likes purple in all shades."

Debbie felt the hair on her nape stand on alert. She picked up a teddy in a light-lilac color and showed it to him. It was one she had been thinking about buying herself. "How about this one?"

"Yes, thanks. I think that's just the thing."

"Do you want me to gift wrap if for you?"

"Please."

Debbie was quick and efficient but fumbled slightly when tying the bow. When she was finished she rang up the sale and handed the man his change. She sighed with relief when he walked out.

She didn't get the time to think over her reaction to the stranger as she was kept busy right up until closing. Her hangover had finally dissipated, and now all she wanted to do was find something to eat and crawl into bed.

She locked up, counted the money in the register, and removed most of her takings. It had been a good day financially, so why wasn't she feeling happy? She set the alarm and locked the back door. She made herself a toasted-cheese sandwich and sipped her fifth black coffee for the day while she ate. She had needed the extra caffeine to get her through the day. She cleaned up and headed for the shower.

Debbie had just stepped from the shower when she heard knocking on the door. She didn't feel up to company right now, so she ignored it. The knocking stopped, and as she pulled on her comfortable, large T-shirt she liked to sleep in when she was feeling down, her phone began to ring. She ignored that, too. Her answering machine would pick up, and she would call back tomorrow. She turned the volume down on her phone before she could hear who was calling and climbed into bed.

She tossed and turned. She had thought since she was tired after a long day and had been suffering from a hangover she would have dropped off to sleep quickly. That wasn't the case. She stared at the ceiling for hours on end, her mind in turmoil. She couldn't seem to decide what to do. Her thoughts went around and around until she was ready to scream with frustration. She threw the bedcovers aside and padded out to her kitchen in bare feet. She was about to flip on the light, but she hesitated when she heard a sound outside her apartment door.

Debbie picked up her bat, which she now kept next to the front door and held her breath while she listened. The noise was strange. It sounded like paper crackling. Then she smelled smoke.

She reached out to the doorknob and snatched her hand away when it burned her skin. She raced to the kitchen, grabbed a pot holder, and ran back to the door. She fumbled with the lock as it burned her fingertips, but she was eventually able to get it open. She used the pot holder to turn the metal knob and jumped back when flames began to push inside. She was stuck. There was no other exit, and she was trapped.

She skirted the flames and slammed the door closed. She reached for her phone and dialed 9-1-1 and placed the receiver to her ear. There was nothing there but silence. Her phone was dead. She dropped the phone and ran to her bedroom. She tipped the contents of her purse on the bed, looking for her cell. It wasn't there.

She tried to remember when she had last seen it and slapped a hand to her forehead when she remembered she had left it next to the cash register in her shop. She had no way to call for help and no way to get out of the burning building.

She slumped down on her bed as tears of fear leaked from her eyes. No, she wasn't about to give in. She had to keep calm and try to think of a way to escape. She stood up and pulled a pair of jeans on and a wool sweater over her shirt. She slipped on her boots and began to check the windows. *Shit, where are the keys to the new locks?* She couldn't remember.

She was so hot and tired. Smoke was everywhere now, and if she didn't get out soon she was going to suffocate. There was only one thing she could do. She was going to have to smash a window and jump. She went into the bathroom off her bedroom, grabbed a large towel, and doused it with water. She wrapped the dripping towel over her head and mouth and ran to the kitchen. The flames were everywhere, and she felt the light hairs on her hands shrivel as she picked up one of the timber chairs and ran back to her room, the only place that didn't have fire in it yet. Only smoke. There was lots of smoke. Her lungs felt tight and clogged, but she didn't let that stop her. She heaved and pushed her bed until it was away from the window. She tugged and ripped the curtains down and threw them on the floor. Her energy was sagging, and she knew she needed more oxygen.

Debbie got down on her hands and knees and then lay flat on the floor on her stomach. She removed the now-dry towel from her mouth and gulped in air. Once she was feeling steady again, not so light-headed, she stood up and began to swing the chair at the glass. Shards exploded out, and she swung the chair again and again, until most of the glass was gone. She pulled the towel from her shoulders, folded it, forming a pad, and placed it over the jagged edges. She climbed up on the window ledge and looked down.

It was a lot farther than she had thought, but she didn't have a choice if she was going to survive. She took a deep breath of clean, fresh air and began to cough. She swayed but reached out and gripped the window frame to steady herself. Then she jumped.

She landed awkwardly and felt pain pierce her right ankle. As she fell forward, she ducked her head and rolled. When she stopped moving, she pushed herself to her hands and knees and crawled away from her burning building.

Now that she was out, reaction began to set in. She was so cold, and her body was shaking. Feeling uncoordinated, she collapsed against the brick wall at the entrance to the alley. Just as she slumped down, a loud explosion permeated the air, and she felt something hit her head. She slid to the ground, unconscious before she finished falling.

* * * *

Britt woke from a dead sleep, uneasy and alert. The first thing he noticed was a hint of smoke in the air. Something was wrong. Sleep forgotten, he got up.

He stepped out onto the veranda. The scent of smoke was stronger out here. Britt paced to the other end of the veranda and looked out. Beyond the trees, in the direction of town, the sky was a hazy orange.

The fire was too far away to make out the flames, but the column of smoke reflected its light. And the direction was clear. His thoughts went to Debbie and her shop. The break-in. Glen Parker.

"Shit. Daniel," Britt roared as he ran back into the house. He dialed Debbie's home phone, but the call wouldn't go through. Britt trusted his instincts. He had been trained to do so. Everything in his body told him to go to Debbie.

His brother met him at the back door, fully dressed. "There's a fire in town. I have a feeling—"

Daniel finished the thought. "Debbie's shop and apartment."

Britt had the truck moving before Daniel had closed the passenger door. Britt had the truck moving before Daniel had closed the passenger door. The tires squealed as he planted his foot on the accelerator and the back end fishtailed as he pushed the truck to the limit.

He pulled the truck to a screeching halt four minutes later. He jumped out of the truck, his knees nearly buckling beneath him when he saw Debbie's shop and her apartment above engulfed in flames. There was no way she could have survived the smoke and flames.

Daniel was already on his phone as he leapt from the passenger's side. "I need paramedics here," he yelled as he ran.

Trying to calm his frantic thoughts, Britt scanned the chaotic scene for some sign of Debbie. Darting dangerously close to the flames, he raced around the side of the building.

At that moment, a loud explosion ripped through the air. Fragments of burning wood and glass arced from the building. Britt squinted against the inferno, watching the debris fall. A piece of wood and plaster fell end over end toward the alley that ran along the back of the building. Britt saw the figure slumped against the wall a moment before the debris struck it. The figure collapsed.

Britt took off at a run and was beside Debbie moments later, his brother at his heels.

She looked so small and fragile lying on the cold, hard concrete. Her face was covered with soot, and she had a cut on the side of her head, which was bleeding profusely, but he could see her breathing.

He heard her moan, and then she began to cough. They were deep, racking coughs as her lungs tried to clear out the smoke, but it was the sweetest sound he'd ever heard. She was still alive. Paramedics were at her side a moment later, and one of the men placed an oxygen mask over her face. He slipped a backboard beneath her, and then he and his partner lifted her onto the portable stretcher.

"Where are you taking her?" Britt asked.

"To the clinic down the street. Since the new owners have taken over, they've expanded the clinic and have a mini hospital on site."

"Okay, I'm coming with you."

"Sir, are you a family member?" the paramedic asked.

"Yes, she's my fiancée and I'm also a deputy marshal," Britt replied as he followed. He didn't give the man a chance to refuse him. He just got into the back of the ambulance after they had Debbie in, and he closed the door. They were at the clinic seconds later.

Britt was thankful the new doctor was already there waiting for them and assumed one of the paramedics had called ahead. He helped get Debbie out of the ambulance and followed her into the office.

The new doctor, Simon Drover, took just enough time to introduce himself, then ignored everyone else as he got to work.

Britt watched as he soaked up the blood from the wound on the side of her head and then took a pair of scissors and clipped the hair away from her scalp. The doctor cleaned the wound with alcohol disinfectant and then began to stitch her skin closed. By the time he had finished Britt counted six sutures and was beside himself with anguish at what Debbie had been through.

He was becoming concerned that she had remained unconscious through her coughing. He was about to question the doctor when he looked down and saw her eyes were finally open. The doctor noticed as well.

"Hi there, Ms. Newsome. I'm Dr. Simon Drover. How are you feeling?"

Debbie began to speak but had to cough instead. Once she had finished her bout, she nodded her head, and Britt cringed when he saw her wince in pain and close her eyes.

"I'm going to keep you in the clinic for the rest of the night and most of tomorrow. You received a head wound which required stitches and your lungs are still affected from smoke inhalation. Is there anyone I can call and inform for you?"

Britt saw Debbie shake her head, and then she closed her eyes. When the doctor moved away to get a bowl of soapy water and a washcloth, he took the opportunity to step up to her bedside.

"Hey, baby, are you okay?" he asked, taking her hand in his. She opened her eyes again, and though they filled with tears, she still gave him a wobbly smile and a nod. She gripped his hand tightly and moved her legs. She winced and cried out with pain, which made more tears spill and leave clean tracks on her soot-covered face. "You're still in pain, aren't you, baby? Is it your head?"

Debbie shook her head slightly and pointed down her leg just as the doctor came back. He must have heard him, because the doctor began to ask her questions.

"Is it your knee? No. Your shin? Okay. Is your ankle or foot hurting?" The doctor picked up Debbie's right foot gently at her nod and examined her foot and ankle. She flinched when he touched her ankle, and Britt had to hold himself back from hitting the man for hurting his woman. He knew he was being irrational since the man was only trying to do his job.

"You have a badly sprained ankle. Let me get an ice pack and then I'll get you cleaned up. How's the head? Any headache or nausea?" Debbie shook her head, and the doctor patted her on the leg. "Good. I'll be right back."

Britt ran his thumb over her hand as he held it. He wanted to pick her up and cradle her in his arms. To be able to hold her would help him settle now that she was okay, but he knew he would cause her pain, so he just continued to hold her hand. She had her eyes closed again. She was only coughing sporadically now, and he knew her lungs were going to be fine.

The doctor was back five minutes later and wrapped Debbie's ankle in an ice pack. He then set about washing the soot from her face. When he finished, Britt knew by her deep, steady breathing that she was asleep.

"Is she going to be all right, Doc?"

"Yes. She'll be fine. She will probably be able to go home first thing in the morning since there seem to be no lasting effects from the head wound. She'll be on crutches for a few days and will feel a bit tired, but she's young, strong, and healthy. One of the paramedics told me you're her fiancé. Will she be going home with you?"

"Yeah, she will."

"Good. She's going to need to have someone with her for the next couple of days. You can come back for her around ten in the morning. Oh, and bring her some clean clothes. I'm sure she'll want to shower and get out of the smoke stench that's currently covering her."

"Thanks, Doc. I appreciate your help," Britt said and offered his hand. He left his woman in the doctor's capable hands and drove back to Debbie's store to find Daniel.

Chapter Ten

Britt got out of his truck and found Daniel talking with Luke Sun-Walker and Damon Osborne as they watched the firefighters battle the fire. He stopped beside them and waited patiently for a lull in conversation.

"How's our girl?" Daniel asked.

"She's going to be fine. The new doctor put six stitches in her head and she has a bad sprain, but she's doing okay."

"Thank God. The fire inspector thinks the flame was started deliberately with accelerants. Whoever the motherfucker was, they started the fire on the stairs to Debbie's apartment. It spread rapidly from there, but he won't know for sure until the fire's out and he starts to investigate," Daniel explained.

"Jesus Christ. How the hell did she get out of there?"

"It looks like she broke her bedroom window and jumped," Sheriff Damon Osborne stated.

"Fuck. She could have broken her neck. How the hell high is that window from the ground?" Britt asked, afraid of the answer.

"About ten feet," Sheriff Luke Sun-Walker answered.

"Holy shit. I'll bet that's how she sprained her ankle. She's lucky she didn't break it," Britt exclaimed.

"When are we taking her home with us?" Daniel asked.

"The new Doc says we can pick her up around ten. I'll call Leah at seven and see if she can pick up some new clothes for Deb. Hopefully she can drop them off at the clinic for her."

"Do you think this has anything to do with that bastard who escaped from prison?" Damon asked.

"Shit. I'm not sure. This doesn't follow his MO. He's never set a fire before. He usually only works with explosives."

"He could have changed it to throw you off," Luke suggested.

"Hm. I just don't know. Maybe once the fire inspector has finished investigating, I'll be able to answer that question. Make sure he gets a copy of Glen Parker's prints," Britt said.

"Will do. Thank God the firefighters were able to contain the blaze and stop it from spreading to the building next door. This whole block could have gone up in smoke. Do you know who called it in?" Britt asked.

"No. Don't you worry, I'll be checking into that, too," Damon stated.

"Why don't you two go home and get some rest? From what I hear your woman's pretty feisty. You're going to need some sleep to be able to deal with her when you get her home," Luke said with a grin.

"Who the hell have you been talking to?" Britt asked.

"Giles was at your woman's place putting in a security system she didn't order. Seems like she was a bit peeved about that. Giles heard her bitching to Leah," Luke stated.

Britt didn't answer. He turned away and headed to the truck. Daniel was following him, and the sound of Luke's laughter carried into the night over the sound of spraying hoses and a diminishing fire.

* * * *

Debbie was sitting up on the bed in a cotton hospital gown when Leah walked into the room. She was glad she had been able to shower and wash away the grime from her body. She hadn't been able to wash her hair due to the sutures and could still smell the lingering scent of smoke. She'd had a bit of trouble since she could only stand on one leg, but in the end she had accomplished what she needed to.

"Debbie. Oh my God. Are you okay? Britt called me this morning and asked me to get you some clothes. He told me what happened. Are you hurt?"

"I'm fine," Debbie replied and winced at the sound of her raspy voice as she hugged Leah.

"You don't sound fine. Your men are going to be here soon. Why don't I help you get dressed? Shit, look at those stitches. Does your head hurt? I hear you sprained your ankle when you jumped out your bedroom window. Why didn't you call for help?" Leah babbled.

"Breathe, Leah. I'm okay, really," Debbie replied as she clung to her friend. Tears spilled over her cheeks, and she sniffed. She didn't want to start crying now, because she was scared if she did, she wouldn't be able to stop.

"You could have died," Leah said, and Debbie heard her voice tremble with emotion.

"Stop it. You're going to make me cry. And who said they are my men?"

Leah pulled away from Debbie and stood with her hands on her hips, glaring down at her. "You can lie to yourself all you want, but we both know they are your men. Now then, let me help you get dressed. I've had to bring you some of my lingerie which I haven't worn yet, and even though I know it will be too big for you at least you know it's good quality."

"Leah, you're not fat. You're not that much bigger than I am. I would be proud to have your figure. Your shape reminds me of Marilyn Monroe. Now, get the ass into gear and help me out of this fashion statement," Debbie said facetiously, plucking at the hospital gown.

Debbie was thankful for Leah's help. She would have been in trouble if she'd had to dress by herself. Her friend made sure the material of the cargo pants didn't touch her swollen, bruised ankle, which she wouldn't have been able to do herself. By the time she was dressed she was feeling tired again. She wanted to lie down and close her eyes, but she conversed with Leah instead. She looked toward the door with trepidation when she heard two heavy sets of steps walking toward the room. She knew Britt and Daniel were walking heavily on purpose. They usually didn't make a sound. Her friend must have seen her uncertainty because she leaned over and took hold of her hand.

"If it doesn't work out, you can come and stay with me."

"Thank you," Debbie replied, and she was very grateful. She had nowhere else to live and no idea what she was going to do. She wasn't sure if she was doing the right thing by going home with Daniel and Britt, but she wasn't going to let the fear of getting hurt stand in her way. She was glad Leah had read her the riot act and called her a coward. It was what she had needed to give her a push in the right direction.

Debbie gave Leah a hug and promised to call, and then she heard Leah greeting Daniel and Britt. She saw Daniel first. He entered the room, rushed over to her, and gave her a fierce hug without hurting her.

"Hi, honey. Are you feeling all right?"

"Yeah, I'm good."

"Are you ready to get out of here?" Daniel asked.

"Yes."

"Are you sure you're okay? You don't sound too good."

"I'm fine, Daniel. My throat is a bit sore and my voice was affected by the smoke," Deb explained.

"Should you be talking then?"

"I promise. I'm fine."

"Hey, baby," Britt said when Daniel moved back from her. "You look tired. Do you want me to carry you so you don't have to use those things?"

Debbie looked at the crutches he indicated and shook her head. She picked them up and began the tedious walk out to their truck. She didn't speak as she concentrated on using the apparatus, but while she moved she contemplated the apology she was going to give them as soon as they got home. She had been a bitch when she had left their house yesterday. *God, was it only yesterday? It feels like a week has passed.*

She was grateful when Britt wrapped an arm around her waist and took her walking aids from her to pass them to Daniel. He held her steady then picked her up in his arms and placed her gently on the backseat. He wouldn't even let her put her own seat belt on. He reached across her and clipped her in. She leaned her back on the headrest with her leg stretched out along the seat. She heard the truck start and felt it move, but her eyelids were too heavy to open. She dozed until the vehicle stopped, and then she unbuckled her belt.

"Stay right where you are, baby. I'll get you out," Britt said, and then he was beside her, the door open. He scooped her up and carried her into the house.

"Thank you," Debbie said as he placed her on the living room sofa.

"No problem, Debs. Do you want something to eat or drink? Do you have any medication for the pain?"

"I would love a cup of coffee, please. I do have pain meds, but I don't need one right now."

"I'll be right back, baby," Britt said and headed for the kitchen.

Debbie was tucked into the corner of the suede sofa with her leg on the couch and a small pillow propping her foot up. She thought about the shop she had worked so hard to get up and running. Just as business was booming, it had burnt to the ground. She was thankful she had insurance, and even though she would be able to replace everything, nothing would be able to replace her personal items she had in her apartment. She'd had her grandmother's wedding and engagement rings in a box on her dressing table. Those rings were irreplaceable.

She had been estranged from her parents and sister for so many years now that she knew they wouldn't have come to help her in a crisis. They had never been able to understand why she wasn't as academic as they were.

Debbie had felt like the poor, orphaned relative with her family. Her parents couldn't seem to understand she was as brainy as they were and didn't want to excel in the world of academia or medicine. In the end, when she had applied for a job as a receptionist when she was first out of school, there had been a big argument, and her parents had washed their hands of her. She had been on her own ever since. Debbie had tried to mend the bridges with her family, but they seemed content to pretend their stupid daughter didn't even exist.

"Here you go, Debs," Britt said and placed her coffee on the table beside her.

Daniel entered the room and sat in the chair opposite the sofa. He looked tired, and she knew it was because of the incident last night. Britt straightened up and turned away, obviously heading for the kitchen again, but she stopped him.

"Could you please sit down for a moment? I'd like to talk to you both."

"Sure, Debs," Britt replied. Debbie waited until he sat on the other end of the sofa, being careful not to touch her foot.

"I want to apologize to you both for leaving the way I did yesterday. I know I hurt you, and I'd like to be able to say it wasn't deliberate, but that would be a lie. I was scared of the way you made me feel." She paused to look at both of them and took a deep breath. "No one has ever made me feel the way you two do. So instead of sitting down like the adult I'm supposed to be and discussing my fears with you, I acted like a child and ran away. I'm so sorry for doing that. I hope you can find it in your hearts to forgive me. I love you both very much."

Debbie lowered her head as tears began to spill over her cheeks. She couldn't look at them and see the rejection on their faces. She felt the sofa move, and then Britt and Daniel were on their knees by her side. They each took one of her hands in theirs, and she gathered her courage to look at them. What she saw in their eyes humbled her. She could see how much they cared for her.

"Baby, I knew you were scared of something, and I knew you were running. I forgave you the moment Daniel drove out the driveway. Yes, it hurt that you didn't sit down and talk to us and ran instead, but I wasn't about to give up. I love you, Debbie. You are the only woman I have ever said those words to, and you will be the only one I will ever say them to," Britt said, his voice much deeper and huskier than normal.

"Honey, you are my world. I would be lost without you. I love your more than words can express. I forgive you. My love for you is unconditional. I don't expect you to say those words in return, because I can see you're not ready yet. But I know deep down that you love me, too. I want you to promise me you will come to one of us if your fears rear their head or you're concerned about something. Haven't you heard the saying a problem shared is a problem halved? Please, promise me you won't run again," Daniel said.

"I promise," Debbie whispered. Her throat and chest were constricted with emotion, and she couldn't speak any louder even if she had wanted to. She pulled Daniel to her and wrapped her arms around his shoulders. She hugged him as tightly as she could. She eventually leaned back and kissed him on the lips then released him. She stared into his eyes and could see the love he had for her. Her heart was so full she couldn't speak.

Her gaze moved to Britt, and she pulled him closer, hugging him fiercely. She could see the sincerity in his eyes and knew she was already in love with both of these special men.

"Thank you for giving me another chance and also for the gift of your hearts. I do have very strong feelings for the both of you, and I know in time I will be able to return those words to you. I promise to take care of the love you give to me freely."

Debbie returned their smile and wiped her wet cheeks. She felt so much emotion she was nearly bursting it with it, and she knew deep down she loved them, too, but she just wasn't ready to say the words yet.

"You look tired, baby. Why don't you nap on the sofa while Daniel and I prepare some lunch?" Britt asked.

He stood up, reached out, and caressed her cheek then headed to the kitchen. Daniel pulled a throw from the back of the sofa and covered her. He bent down and kissed her on the forehead before he followed his brother out of the room.

Debbie leaned back and closed her eyes. They were still sore from the smoke, and she knew she probably looked a mess. Her hair had been cut away in a patch, and she had stitches in the side of her head. What surprised her though was her head didn't give her any pain at all, but her ankle was throbbing like a bitch. She knew she was probably due for another pain reliever, but she couldn't be bothered to get up to go into the kitchen on her crutches, which her men had thoughtfully placed on the floor within easy reach. So she just sat there trying to relax. Her thoughts returned to her parents and sister, but this time she smiled. It had been a long time since she felt like part of a family, but as she listened to the deep rumble of Britt's and Daniel's voices as they made lunch in the kitchen, she felt that was about to change.

Chapter Eleven

Deb scratched at her newly healed skin as she drove to the sheriff's department. Having the stitches out was nearly as pleasant as not being on crutches anymore, she thought, but neither was going to be as amazing as finally being able to wash her hair. Since the fire a week ago, she had been spraying her tresses with a leave-in conditioner, but she swore she could still smell the lingering scent of smoke.

As the sheriff's department came into sight, her heart lifted more. Her men were there. She was becoming so dependent on them being there, and that scared her a little, but she wouldn't give them up for anything in the world. Solicitous to the point of ludicrousness, they had nursed her through a week of boring convalescence, and though Debbie was still unsure what would become of her business, she wanted the brothers to figure in her life.

The only thing that bothered her was that she knew they were hiding something from her. Over the last few days, she had walked in on the two brothers' conversations and they had stopped talking and had looked uncomfortable. She knew they would eventually talk to her if they wanted her know what was going on.

She pulled the borrowed truck into a parking space and got out. She turned and scanned the street when she felt the hair at her nape stand up, but she shrugged off her paranoia when she didn't see anyone looking her way.

She climbed the steps and entered the building. A dark-haired woman rose from a desk near the back of the room and walked up to the counter to greet her.

"Hi, how can I help you?"

"I'm here to see Britt and Daniel, if they're not too busy."

"Oh, you must be Debbie, I'm Rachel. I've heard so much about you, I feel like we've already met," Rachel said.

"Um, well, thanks, Rachel. Sorry, but I haven't heard about you," Debbie replied and gave her a wry smile.

Rachel laughed and moved to open the small gate separating the room. "Come on through. I'm sorry about what happened to your home and shop. I can't believe I didn't get the chance to see your stuff. I had planned on it this coming weekend, but I guess it doesn't matter, as long as you're safe and well. Do you want a cup of coffee? Your men are in a meeting with Luke and Damon at the moment. They shouldn't be too much longer."

"Thanks, that would be nice," Deb replied. "So, I can't believe I've never seen you before. How long have you worked here?"

"Oh, about six months now. It was fate," Rachel said, and Debbie saw the dreamy smile on her face and her unfocused eyes. "I was on the run from my ex-boss and when I arrived here I had no cash left. I applied for the job as an administration assistant here and the rest, as they say, is history. Oh, you should come to the Slick Rock Hotel one night. We could have a girls' night out or something. One of my men, Tyson, owns and runs the place."

"You have more than one man, too? God, what is it about this town that draws women to men, like bees to flowers? Do you know Leah?" Debbie asked.

"Sure. She had a crush on my Damon for a while there, but she's happy with her own men now. They treat her so sweetly, so do my men. I have three. You've already met Damon of course, and then there's Tyson and then my Sam. Shit, I've got to stop thinking about them. I get sappy and horny every time I do." Rachel sighed. "So, are you going to open up your shop again?"

"I haven't decided yet. I loved having the shop while I did, and it seemed to fill a need in me, but I don't know what I want anymore,"

Deb replied. Her insurance company had come through, but she didn't know if she was going to spend the time to get her business up and running again. It had been a lot of hard work, and even though she was becoming bored, she knew how much work was ahead of her if she was to start her shop once more.

"Oh yeah. I hear you, girlfriend. You've used your business to fill that empty hole in your heart, and now that you're in love with two sexy men, that emptiness has gone."

Debbie felt the blood drain from her face. She placed her mug of coffee on the desk so that it didn't fall from her trembling hand. She had known she had strong feelings for her men, and even knew she might be in love with them, but to have a stranger peg her so quickly was very disconcerting.

"I'm sorry," Rachel said quietly and patted Deb on the hand. "Did I say something wrong?"

"No. I...I...Shit. I knew I was falling in love with them, but I didn't realize I was using my business to fill holes in my life. To have it pointed out so clearly was a bit of a shock. I can remember my parents berating me as a child. They often asked me what I wanted to do with my life and my answer was always the same. To get married and have babies. Of course to them that was utter sacrilege. I was supposed to want to have a career like they did. They're both very high up in the academic world and my older sister is one of the top neurosurgeons in the country. I tried so hard to win their love and affection, but I don't think they ever knew the real me and they never stopped to try and understand me. I was considered the black sheep of the family." Debbie paused and inhaled deeply. "You know, I think I'd really like to have a night out. When would you like to go?"

"How about tonight, since it's Friday? Your parents were very shortsighted and selfish. Don't let their shortcomings affect your hopes and dreams. Stand up for what you want out of life and grab onto it with both hands. Life's too short not to. I was like you. Too scared to see what was under my nose and too busy trying to protect everyone else. But you know what? I was wrong, and I now have three men who love me and I love in return. Don't let fear and other people's opinions stop you from going after what you want," Rachel stated.

"Shit, I've been such an idiot," Deb grumbled.

"Who called you an idiot?" Britt's voice boomed across the room.

Debbie looked up to see Britt and Daniel walking toward her as well as the two sheriffs, Luke and Damon.

"No one," Debbie said with a shrug.

"Give me a look at your head," Britt said. Debbie tried not to shiver as he ran his fingers through her hair and smoothed over the pink scar on her scalp. Just a touch or a look from him or Daniel was enough to turn her to mush. She had it so bad. "It doesn't look too horrid, baby. Your hair covers it and no one will ever know it was even there."

"What are you doing here, honey?" Daniel asked. He placed a hand on her shoulder and gave her a slight rub.

"I thought if you weren't too busy, we could have lunch together at the diner. But I understand if you can't."

"No, we're finished here for the moment. Let's go, baby." Britt helped her to her feet by placing a hand at her elbow.

"Oh, I nearly forgot. Rachel's invited me out to the hotel tonight. Do you mind if I go?"

"How about we all go?" Damon asked. "We can have a meal and then listen to the new band Tyson's hired on."

"That sounds perfect. You can call Sam and Tyson and let them know we're going out. Tyson's going to have to keep our table free and add another to it for the evening," Rachel responded.

"Okay, we'll see you there around seven. I'm really looking forward to it, Rachel. Thank you," Debbie said, and then she took Daniel's and Britt's hands in hers and led them from the office.

"You seem happy, honey. Are you glad you got your stitches out?" Daniel asked.

"You have no idea. I can't wait to get home and wash my hair."

"You don't have to have lunch with us if you want to go home, baby," Britt said.

"I know, but I want to be with you both. I missed you."

Britt stopped on the sidewalk and turned her to face him. She looked him square in the eye and let him see her emotions. She heard his breath catch and knew he could see her love for him shining from her eyes. She turned her head to Daniel and let him see how much she loved him, too.

"You sure pick your moments, baby," Britt whispered, and then his mouth was on hers. The fact that she was standing on the sidewalk faded into the background. She opened her mouth up to his when his tongue licked along her lips and kissed him with all her pent-up emotions. When he pulled back they were both breathing heavily.

"My turn," Daniel rasped and pulled her into his arms. He devoured her, sliding his tongue along hers, and she couldn't prevent a moan from escaping. She jumped and pulled away when she heard a car horn blast.

"Come on, we'd better go eat before we give the fine citizens of Slick Rock something to gossip about," Debbie said, holding their hands again, and began to walk.

"Would it bother you, Debs?" Britt asked.

"Would what bother me?"

"Being the object of gossip?"

"No. I don't care what anyone thinks. I love you both too much to worry about pusillanimous, small-minded people. If they have nothing better to do with their lives then that's their problem, not mine."

"Honey, you are so sexy when you're preachy. No, you're just downright sexy all the time. I love you, too, Deb," Daniel replied. "You've made me very happy by saying you love us."

"Stop it. You're going to make me cry."

"Love you, baby," Britt whispered in her ear.

"Me, too," Deb replied and then had to clear her throat. "Okay, let's get some lunch. I'm hungry."

While they ate they sat chatting about what she was going to do about her business and about the other ménage relationships in Slick Rock. She hadn't realized Luke was also in the same sort of relationship and wanted to meet the woman who could tame the large, wild-looking sheriff. She was thinking of planning a barbecue and inviting Leah and her men, Rachel and hers, and Luke and his woman and friends. She was glad she wasn't the only woman in town in an unconventional relationship. It made her feel more at ease.

Once lunch was over, her men walked her back to the truck, kissed her good-bye, and sent her on her way home. They would be home around five o'clock so they could get ready for their night out.

She planned to try and get a little loving with her men before they went out for dinner. She'd only been with them the one time, and now that she was one hundred percent healthy again, she needed to feel the touch of the men she loved.

Chapter Twelve

"Honey, we're home. Where are you?" Daniel called as soon as he entered the back door. He had been itching to have Debbie in his arms since lunchtime. His heart was so full with joy and love, and he wanted to show her just how much he needed her. He had waited too long for her to say she loved him, and now that she had, he wanted to make love with her. His cock had been hard for hours, and he wanted to lose himself in her sweet body.

"I'm in my bedroom," she called out.

Daniel hurried down the hallway and then froze at her bedroom door. She had candles lit all around the room, their flames flickering and their scent wafting to his nostrils. But what drew and held his attention was the sight of his woman lying on the bed amongst a heap of pillows, with the covers on the bed pulled down, and totally, gloriously naked.

He drew in a breath and stepped farther into the room. He didn't look at Britt when his brother gasped behind him. He just stared at her while he removed his clothes. When he was standing before her nude, he clasped his cock in his hand and pumped his shaft. She just continued to stare at him, her eyes roving over his body, and her cheeks beginning to flush with arousal. He loved the fact that he could get her horny without touching her. He let his cock go and moved to her side on the bed.

"I love you, honey," he whispered and then took her mouth with his.

He groaned as he slid his tongue between her lips and tasted every inch of her sweet, moist cavern. He placed his hand on her belly and smoothed his palm up over her soft, silky, warm skin. When he got to her breast, he used his fingers to frame the fleshy mound, withdrew his mouth from hers, and kissed his way down her throat to her chest. He laved his tongue over her dusky pink nipple and then sucked it into his mouth. She cried out with pleasure, and his cock jerked with need. He released her turgid peak, and then he kissed, licked, and nibbled his way down her body.

Daniel placed a leg between hers and nudged her thighs apart. He lifted his head and looked at the love of his life. Her chest and cheeks were flushed, her pink nipples were hard, and she was currently kissing his brother, who was now naked and on the bed at her side. He saw her reach out and wrap her hand around Britt's cock. Her small white hand pumping his brother's dick was so damned erotic, his cock jerked.

He slid his hands beneath her ass and massaged the firm, fleshy globes as he lowered his head. He growled when her cream coated his tongue as he licked her from anus to clit and back again. He rimmed his tongue around her wet pussy hole and then thrust it into her body. When he looked up the length of her body, he nearly shot his load. He gripped his balls and gave them a firm tug to prevent himself from coming too soon. His woman suckled on his brother's cock. Her lips were red and full, stretched wide around his brother's shaft as she bobbed along his length.

Daniel's control was slipping, and even though they only had a limited amount of time, he wanted to make his woman come before he entered her body and made love to her. Closing his eyes again, he concentrated on bringing his Debbie pleasure. He eased two fingers into her cunt and lapped at her clit. He smiled against her flesh as she bucked her hips up, begging him for more. When he found her sweet spot, he slid the pads of his fingers over her again and again. Caging her clit between his teeth, he laved his tongue over the sensitive bundle of nerves, over and over. He made sure not to lift his tongue away from her clit and was rewarded when she cried out and grabbed hold of his hair with her hand.

Her walls fluttered and rippled around his digits, and he knew his love was close to orgasm. He changed the angle of his fingers and made sure he pumped his fingers deep and fast, caressing over her G-spot with every pass. He loved the sounds she made when they pleasured her. He felt her flesh clamp down on his digits, and she screamed as she climaxed.

He withdrew his fingers from her hole, placed his tongue at her entrance, and lapped up her juices. She tasted so exquisite he didn't want to miss a drop of her cum. When the last quiver died away, he sat up, swiped a hand over his chin and mouth, and moved in closer to her.

He began to ease his cock into her body while he watched her give Britt a blow job. He groaned as her tight, wet flesh enveloped him. He had found heaven on earth. To be able to tell Debbie he loved her freely and have her return those sentiments was magical. To be able to hold her in his arms and love her with his body was special. He was halfway in her body, and sweat was running down his face as he held his control on a tight leash. He wanted to surge into her until he was embedded in her body balls-deep, but he didn't want to hurt her. But she surprised him by taking the matter in her own hands, so to speak. She lifted her hips up and forward until he could feel his cock touching against her womb. She released Britt's cock with a slurp and a pop and reached both hands out toward him.

"I love you both, so much. Please. I need you to love me at the same time," Debbie panted out.

"Come here then, honey," Daniel said breathlessly and gently pulled her up onto his lap and into his arms. "God, I love you so much, Deb. I want to love and hold you forever. Just relax those muscles and let Britt stretch you."

Daniel took her mouth and swept his tongue inside hers. The fact that she kissed him back with equal fervor, when he knew she would be able to taste her own juices on his tongue, just made him eager for more of her. When the need for oxygen necessitated movement, he lifted his head and leaned his chin on her shoulder, watching his brother prepare their woman for some double loving. He held her firmly so she couldn't wriggle around too much and hurt herself.

Britt massage lubed fingers over the skin of her ass, and then pushed two fingers into her back hole. His cock jumped inside her at the erotically dark, carnal sight. His brother withdrew his digits from her ass, and then he moved in closer to Debbie.

Daniel moved his cock back, giving Britt room to move, and then her pussy tightened on his erection as his brother entered her ass. Her pelvic-floor muscles rippled around him and then stilled when his sibling was in her anus to the hilt. He held on to her hips and pulled back, his cock sliding along her wet sheath. As he slowly surged back in, Britt pulled out of her anus. Daniel wanted to go gently and slowly, to savor loving his woman, but he didn't think he could. He could already feel his balls roiling, wanting to spill his seed inside of her.

"Please, you have to fuck me," Debbie cried out.

"We are, baby," Britt growled.

"No. Yes. It's so good. I want more. I need you to love me at the same time. Fast and hard."

Daniel ground his teeth and clenched his jaw. He waited for Britt to surge back into her ass, and when his bother began to pull out, so did he. They thrust their hips fast and hard, filling and retreating at the same time. The animalistic sounds Debbie made as they fucked her were music to his ears.

"Oh yes. That's so good. I'm so close," Debbie sobbed.

Daniel kept pace with Britt as they pounded in and out of her body. Their flesh slapped together, and he surged harder and faster. He advanced and retreated, in and out of her pussy over and over again. Her cunt walls got tighter and tighter, and he knew she was close. His balls drew up as the tingle at the base of his spine grew stronger. He reached down between them and gently squeezed her clit between finger and thumb as he pumped his hips.

She tilted her head back, her breath hitched in her lungs, and then she keened as her pussy clamped down on his cock, bathing his erection with her juices as she shook and contracted continually around him. Her sheath milked the cum from his balls, and he shouted as he spewed his seed into her body. He heard his brother's roar as he, too, fell over the threshold into bliss.

He wrapped Debbie in his arms and held her as she slumped down onto him, trusting him to support her weight. The three of them breathing harshly was the only sound in the room.

Debbie stirred, and he loosened his hold on her. She groaned as Britt moved from behind her and then kissed her on the shoulder as he stood up.

"We'd better get a move on, baby. We have to get cleaned up and we only have half an hour before we're supposed meet the others at the hotel. Come on, Deb." Britt offered her his hand. "I'll help you wash."

"Oh no. You two had better use the other bathroom, otherwise we'll never get out of here," she replied with a smile.

Daniel picked her up in his arms and slid from her body. He carried her into her bathroom and placed her on her feet. He held her at the waist until he was sure she was steady on her feet, kissed her lightly on the lips, and left the room.

* * * *

Debbie was glad to have found another woman she got on with. She and Rachel chatted like they were old friends. They had all enjoyed a meal, and now they were sitting around two tables which had been put together near the bar and dance floor. She had met all of Rachel's men and knew why the girl had a permanent smile on her face. She had three hunky men slathering her with love and attention.

The men talked amongst themselves while she and Rachel spoke. Rachel had suggested, since Debbie didn't know if she wanted the responsibility of another shop, that she should start an online business to sell her lingerie instead.

She thought that was a great idea. She could use the spare room above the garage to store her merchandise until the items were bought and ready to ship. There was plenty of room for her to set up her business without any of her stuff taking over the house.

"You're brilliant, Rachel. I'm so glad to have you for a friend," Debbie said, reaching over to give Rachel's hand a pat.

"Hey, we women have to stick together, you know. We'd be drowning in testosterone if we didn't."

"Oh, very true."

"You'd better watch it, sugar, or you might find yourself over my knee," Tyson retorted, and Debbie looked up to see him giving Rachel a wicked grin.

"Do you promise?" Rachel asked breathlessly.

"Cut it out, you two," Damon said, but Debbie saw him give Rachel a wink.

"Oh my," Debbie said, fanning her hot face with her hand. "I think I need another drink."

"What do you want, baby?" Britt asked, already rising to his feet.

"I'll have another Pinot, please."

"Does anyone else want a drink?" Britt asked then headed to the bar with the orders.

The band started to play one of Debbie's favorite songs, "With Arms Wide Open" by Creed. She grabbed Rachel's hand and pulled her along to the dance floor.

"I absolutely love this song," Debbie said and started to dance.

"I do, too," Rachel replied.

Debbie danced to the music, letting the beat and melody wash over her. She lost herself in the lyrics and let her body flow uninhibitedly and naturally.

By the end of the night, Debbie knew she had found more great friends and planned to have the barbecue the following weekend. As they were leaving the hotel, she told Rachel to bring her men out the following Saturday afternoon and followed her men to the truck.

When they got home Deb put the coffeepot on and waited for it to brew. Her men followed her into the kitchen and sat at the table waiting for a cup.

"Debbie, we have something we need to tell you," Daniel stated.

"Okay, just let me get the coffee and I'll be with you," she replied. Debbie had a sinking feeling in her gut and was scared about what they wanted to discuss, but instead of running she was facing everything head-on now. She placed their mugs on the table and went back for her own. She went to sit in the seat between them, but Daniel pulled her onto his lap.

"You know we work for the government and are special operatives. But we have made some enemies along the way. Baby, we think one the men we helped put into prison is on his way here. He escaped, and we've had word that he is heading in this direction," Britt explained.

"Okay. Do the sheriffs know to keep an eye out?" Debbie asked.

"Yes, they do. We want you to be more vigilant. This bastard is a real sicko and works with explosives."

"What sort of explosives? Do you mean like bombs?" Debbie whispered, chills racing up and down her spine.

"Yes, honey," Daniel replied. "He blames us for his family leaving him. His wife and child haven't been near him since he was caught."

"Well, shit. I don't blame them. That poor woman must have been terrified," Debbie said.

"Yeah, but the thing is, baby, he vowed to get back at us and we think he may come after you," Britt explained.

"You think he set the fire, don't you?" Debbie asked in a whisper.

"We're not sure, honey. Fire isn't his usual MO, but who's to say he hasn't changed the way he works," Daniel said.

"We aren't telling you this to scare you, baby. We just want you to be more alert. We don't know for sure if he knows where we are, but my gut is telling me he's coming, if he's not already here," Britt said. "I don't want you going anywhere without your cell phone. I have already programmed our numbers on speed dial for you. We would prefer if you stayed in the house and didn't venture out on your own."

"We will keep you safe, honey. We have been trained and can hide in shadows and no one ever seems to realize we are there. We have black belts in karate and we can speak to each other with our own brand of sign language," Daniel explained.

"Well, that certainly explains things."

"What does, baby?" Britt asked.

"I felt like I was being watched lots of times. Each time I looked out the shop window no one was there. It kind of gave me the creeps," Debbie stated.

"Sorry, honey. We didn't know you could feel us. We didn't want to scare you or make you feel bad," Daniel replied.

"Wait," Britt interrupted. "How often have you felt like you were being watched, Debs?"

"I'm not sure. Let me think," Debbie said and tried to remember how many times she felt like she was being watched. "From what I can remember, it probably would have been five or six times."

Daniel and Britt looked to each other in a near-identical movement. They were silent for three or four seconds, but something seemed to pass between them. A series of tiny muscle movements—the tick of Britt's right eye, the locking and releasing of Daniel's jaw—made her think back to what Daniel had just told her about their sign language.

Whatever was going on, they didn't look happy.

"What?" Debbie asked nervously and clutched Daniel's arm. "Just tell me what's happening."

"I think Glen Parker, the man who escaped from prison, is already here," Britt said and took her hand in his.

"Oh God. Do you think we should leave?" Debbie asked, feeling the blood drain from her face.

"No, baby. If this motherfucker is coming after us, then that's good. We'll be able to recapture him and make sure he is incarcerated for the rest of his natural life. We have Luke and Damon on the lookout as well as Damon's brothers. They are all highly trained ex-Marines and they know what he looks like," Britt explained.

"We've got the best security system in this place as well as the room over the garage. I want you to make sure you keep the alarm on at all times, but especially when you're here alone. We have the alarm system set up to call our phones if it's tripped. If you ever feel unsafe all you have to do is call," Daniel stated.

"Will you guys sleep with me tonight? You've sort of made me nervous," Debbie admitted.

"Baby, we have just been waiting for you to ask us that. We have wanted to be in your bed from the first. We made sure your bedroom was decorated the way you liked it and planned to share it with you from day one. We just wanted to make sure it was what you wanted. So yes, we will sleep with you and continue to do so from this night on, but if you ever feel the need to have the bed to yourself for a night, don't hesitate in letting us know. We understand that you may need some space of your own now and then," Britt explained.

"Britt?"

"Yeah, baby?"

"Shut up, take me to bed, and love me."

"Your wish is my command, Debs," Britt replied.

He scooped her up in his arms and carried her to her room. She looked over his shoulder to see Daniel waggling his eyebrows at her as he followed.

Chapter Thirteen

Britt placed Debbie onto the edge of the mattress and knelt down on the floor in front of her. He leaned in and lightly nibbled on her lower lip and then sucked it into his mouth. His cock filled and hardened more when he felt her hands sift through his hair. He released her lip and swept his tongue into her mouth. He groaned with approval as she dueled with him and then sucked on his flesh. He slowed the kiss and moved back so he could look into her eyes as he undressed her.

He pushed the dress off her shoulders and sucked air into his lungs when he caught sight of her. His cock throbbed against the constriction of his pants when he saw what she was wearing. She had on black thigh-high stockings, which were attached to a garter belt, and her high heels. And nothing else.

"Baby, if I had known what you were wearing, or weren't wearing, under that dress we would never have left the house," he rasped.

"Why do you think I didn't tell you?" she replied in a low, husky voice.

Britt couldn't take any more. He ripped his clothes off, not caring that buttons flew from his shirt, and when he was naked he picked her up, placed her in the middle of the bed, and rolled with her. He made sure not to crush her, but arched his hips up to hers when she was finally lying on top of him. He loved the sensation of having her warm skin against his. He could feel her nipples poking into his chest, and her cream leaked from her pussy, coating his hard cock.

He moaned when she wiggled her hips and her wet flesh slid over his erection. He cupped the back of her head with his hand, gripping her hair lightly, and tilted her face up to his. Their lips met in a slow, loving kiss, but it quickly turned to hot and carnal. He slipped his tongue along hers and then over her teeth, cheek, and the roof of her mouth. He couldn't get enough of her taste. He wanted to taste every single, delectable inch of her body. He wanted to crawl beneath her skin, embedding himself into her heart and soul, and never leave.

He weaned his mouth from hers and helped her to sit up on his stomach. She looked like a goddess with her hair spilling around her shoulders and down her back. Her breasts were lush and perky, tipped with her dusky pink nipples. He kneaded her breasts and pinched her turgid peaks and let them go again when she clutched his arms.

"I want you inside me," Debbie whispered.

Britt used his considerable strength and lifted her with ease. He growled when she took hold of his cock and placed it at the entrance to her cunt. She pushed down onto him, and his flesh slid into her wet heat until the head touched her womb.

"Love me," Debbie sobbed out. "Please love me and never stop."

"We won't, baby. Come down here so Daniel can get his dick in your ass. We are going to love you so long and so good, Debs. We'll never let you go. You belong here, in our bed, our home, and our hearts," Britt said, overwhelmed by emotion.

"God, you two are so sweet. I can't believe you love me. I love you both so much. You're more than I deserve."

"Wrong, honey. You're perfect for us. I love you, too. You're embedded in my heart and soul for always," Daniel said.

Even Britt could hear the emotion behind the words his sibling said to their woman. He slid his hands down her body and held the cheeks of her ass wide for his brother. He knew Daniel was preparing Debbie for his cock because she shifted on him and her pussy clenched and released around him. He just wished Daniel would hurry the hell up because he was eager to begin giving their woman the pleasure she deserved.

"I'm in," Daniel growled.

"About fucking time," Britt replied.

"Stop arguing, children, and love me," Debbie said with a giggle, which quickly turned to a moan as Britt pulled his cock back to just inside the entrance of her pussy.

"Oh yes. That's so good," Debbie mewed.

"It's about to get a whole lot better, honey," Daniel replied.

Britt pushed his hips up, gliding his cock back into her as he held Debbie above him with his hands on her rib cage. As he pulled out again, Daniel thrust forward and filled her ass with his hard rod. They set up a slow pace, not wanting to go too fast and hard and have their loving end too soon. Debbie clutched his biceps as he withdrew and pushed back in again. He and Daniel slid their erections in and out of her holes in counterthrusts to the other, making sure she was filled with one of them at all times. He lifted his head and sucked one of her nipples into his mouth. He suckled on her with strong pulls, knowing how much she loved to have her peaks stimulated while they fucked her.

Time and space had no meaning as he concentrated on giving their woman pleasure. The sounds she made and the rippling of her body filled his senses. He knew by the escalating pace of her breathing that she was getting close to the edge. He released her nipple with a pop and slid his mouth over to the other one, not wanting it to feel neglected. He laved the elongated tip with his tongue and drew it into his mouth. He scraped the edge of his teeth over her flesh and chuckled when she cried out. He switched from tip to tip until she was writhing between him and his brother, sobbing for the completion only they could give her.

And then she surprised him again. She used her pelvic-floor muscles, tightening and releasing around his hard cock. The little minx was trying to make him lose control, and it was working. Sweat began to roll down his face, and he clenched his jaw. He looked up to see Daniel was in the same predicament. He and Daniel didn't want her taking over this time.

He looked up to see Daniel was in the same predicament. He and Daniel didn't want her taking over this time.

While Debbie was distracted, he sent a coded sign message to Daniel using his facial muscles.

"She's trying to push us over."

Daniel replied in kind. *"I know."*

"Help me pick her up."

"Why did you guys get so quiet?" Debbie gasped.

"Hang on, Deb, we are going to make you feel so good," Daniel rumbled.

"You already are," Debbie sobbed.

With Daniel's help, Britt rose up from the bed and held her between them, without once sliding out of her body. It took some careful maneuvering, but they managed it. Britt had her legs hooked over his arms, and wide open. And by the positioning of Daniel's arms, he held her by her ass cheeks.

"What are you doing?" Deb asked breathlessly.

"We're loving you, baby. Hook your arms around my neck instead of holding my shoulders. Good girl. Now, just relax and let us take care of you," Britt crooned.

The time for slow was over. He and Daniel started out easy, but increased their pace incrementally with every forward thrust of their hips. They still moved in counteraction to each other, making sure their lover was filled with one of their cocks at all times.

"Ooh, that's so good. You're so deep I can nearly feel you in my throat," Debbie sighed.

Britt was at the end of his control. He withdrew and surged back into her pussy over and over again. He looked down as one of Daniel's hands pinched one of her nipples. She arched her neck and rested the back of her head on his brother's shoulder. Daniel leaned over and kissed her as he pushed in and out of Debbie's anus.

Britt felt her pussy walls ripple over his cock and knew she was close. He pumped his hips harder, faster, and deeper, his earlier rhythm shot to hell, and felt a warm tingle at the base of his spine. He kept his eyes on her and watched her face as she drew closer and closer to the edge. He was grunting now as he shuttled his cock in and out of her cunt. Their rhythm lost, he and Daniel thrust wildly, now filling her at the same time, now alternating. Then she was there.

She screamed loud and long as her pussy clamped down and released, over and over again, bathing his cock in her juices. His legs shook from so much pleasure, and he could feel his balls drawing up against his body. He was vaguely aware of his brother yelling and knew he had reached his climax with Debbie. His cock quivered and jerked, and he roared as his cum spewed from the end of his penis in short, sharp bursts.

Once, twice, three and four times, until his balls were completely empty of his seed. He felt so satiated and weak he slid down to the floor, taking Debbie and Daniel with him. He released her legs, and then, with trembling hands, he caressed over her shoulders and down her arms, hugging her to him. Her muscles were lax, and her eyes were closed. She looked like she had passed out. He'd never felt so weak yet so fulfilled and complete in his life. She was made just for them, and he was going to do everything within his power to keep her safe and happy.

When his strength had returned and his breathing had slowed, he picked Debbie up and carried her to the bathroom. He sat down on the rim of the tub and turned the faucets on. She was cuddled up in his arms all soft and warm and looked like she was asleep. He sat in the filling tub, lifted her onto his lap, and began to wash her. She gave a drowsy moan, opened her eyes, and looked up at him.

"How did we get in here?"

"I carried you, baby."

"Oh, the last I remember we were on the floor. God, you loved me into oblivion," Debbie whispered with awe.

"We'll do that to you every time we love you if you like it, honey," Daniel rumbled as he entered the bathroom.

"Do you even have to ask?" Deb enquired, and she gave them a saucy wink.

"No, I guess not," Daniel replied.

Debbie yawned, and her eyelids began to close, as if they were too heavy to keep open. He washed her with Daniel's help and then lifted her from the tub. He let her legs slide down until her feet were on the bathmat and held her steady while Daniel dried her off. By the time he climbed into bed beside his lover, she was already asleep.

"She's so special, isn't she, Britt?"

"Yeah, she is. I just hope we can keep her out of danger. My gut is telling me that bastard is already here and planning something," Britt replied.

"I feel it, too. Maybe we should get one of the Alcott brothers here to guard her during the day."

"I think that's a great idea. They're ex-cops, so they know what they're doing. I'll call Giles first thing in the morning and arrange something with him."

"Good. I'll feel a lot better if she has someone looking out for her when we can't be with her. Let's get some shut-eye. Morning comes way too soon," Daniel admitted.

Britt pushed his worries aside for the moment and let sleep take him, too. He was so happy to have Debbie in his bed. He would do everything he could to make sure she was kept safe.

Chapter Fourteen

Debbie opened her eyes and saw her men had already left the bed. She got up, pulled her robe on, and headed to the kitchen. She sighed when she found the room empty but saw the note propped up against the coffeepot.

Sorry you had to wake up alone, baby. We had to head into work for a while. We should be back around lunchtime. If you see Giles, Remy, or Brandon, offer them a cup of coffee. We have one of the Alcott brothers looking out for you while we're not there. I armed the alarm. Keep it on! Love, Britt and Daniel.

Debbie poured herself some coffee and sighed after the first sip. Her men were so sweet when they went all protective and he-man on her. She loved that they cared for her and tried to keep her safe. She made some toast and finished her first mug of coffee, then refilled her cup and took her breakfast to the table. She had just finished eating when she heard a noise at the front of the house. She got up to investigate.

She froze in horror when she saw a lilac teddy taped to the glass with *"boom you're dead"* written on the material in what looked like red paint. Her hand trembled as she placed it over her mouth. She was shocked to see that familiar piece of lingerie, and then her skin crawled as goose bumps rose up over her body. She knew what the escaped convict looked like. She had served him in her shop.

She spun on her heel and ran toward her bedroom where her purse and cell phone were. She scanned the room frantically, but couldn't find her purse. She grabbed some clothes and locked herself in the bathroom. She dressed quickly then rummaged around in the drawers and cupboards looking for a weapon. Shit, there was nothing she could use. She didn't even have a can of deodorant to spray in his eyes, because she used roll-on. Going back in her mind, she tried to remember where she had left her bag the previous night. She had gone straight to the kitchen to brew some coffee.

She unlocked the door and stopped in her room to pull some socks and sneakers on. When she reached the kitchen, she spied her purse sitting in the middle of the dining room table. She backed away from it. Her purse hadn't been there when she had been eating breakfast in here.

Someone behind her spoke. "Hello, sweetness. No, don't turn around," he said. She bit her lip when he pushed something hard into her back. "Put your hands behind your back."

"I know who you are. Why are you doing this, Glen? I have nothing to do with any of this."

"That may be, but your men need to pay. They made my life a living hell by sending me away. Do you know how many people have tried to kill me since I was put in prison? Nearly fifty fucking dirtbags have tried to stab me, choke me, or hang me. My wife and kid won't have a bar of me. Your lovers are going to be held accountable for what they've done," he whispered in a furious voice.

Debbie whimpered with fear when she felt handcuffs click and slide around her wrists. With her arms behind her back, she only had the use of her legs and head. She was so scared that she had broken out in a cold sweat and her whole body was shaking. She wondered if one of the Alcott brothers was really outside and, if so, why they hadn't seen this sicko getting into the house.

"How did you get in without tripping the alarm?"

"Oh, that was simple, sweetness," he replied as he turned her around to face him for the first time since he'd entered the house. "I've been rigging alarms for a long while now. None of them have beaten me yet. Now, let's stop with the chitchat and head into the living room. I have a nice surprise for you."

Debbie knew it was useless to resist. He was so much taller and stronger than she was. She was going to conserve her energy until she really needed it. She wasn't going down without a fight, and if she did have to go down, she was going to make sure she took this bastard with her. No one was going to hurt her men, not if she could help it.

He pointed a gun in her direction and began to give her orders. "See that lovely jacket on the sofa? Pick it up and put it on. Now!"

Debbie turned her head and saw the life jacket. Her teeth began chattering when she saw what looked like plastic explosives and wires on it.

"Hurry up, princess, or I'll just shoot you now."

"I c–can't put it on. You have m–my hands cuffed."

"Shit. Come here, bitch."

Debbie moved two steps closer to him and stopped. She didn't want to move another step.

"Turn around."

She turned immediately when he barked at her and tried to stop her body from shaking, but she couldn't. He took the cuffs off, and then he shoved her toward the sofa. She picked up the jacket and slipped her arms through the holes. She didn't do up the clips though. She wanted to be able to get it off in a hurry if at all possible.

"Now sit in the armchair," he commanded and pushed her.

Debbie sat down and tried not to make any noise as he tied her to the chair securely with rope. He stepped back and gave her an evil smile and then produced the handcuffs and restrained her again.

"Good, now all we have to do is wait. I saw that nice note your lovers left you. They'll be back in a few hours, and boy, are they in for a nice surprise. I think I'll get me some coffee and food while we're waiting. Do you want anything, princess? Oh no, of course you don't. You can't use your hands, can you, sweetness?" he asked facetiously and left the room.

Debbie looked around for something, anything she thought would help get her out of this. She slumped, tears pricking her eyes, and she accepted she couldn't do anything now. She was trussed up like a Thanksgiving turkey, strapped to enough firepower to go up like the Fourth of July. She turned her head cautiously when she caught movement from her peripheral vision. There, peeking into the window, was Remy Alcott. He placed a finger over his lips, telling her to keep quiet. She gave a slight nod of her head, affirming his command, and then he was gone again. Though he didn't reappear, she continued to stare out the window, hoping Remy had contacted the sheriff's department to let them know she was being held captive. She just hoped Britt and Daniel would stay back until she was safe. She couldn't stand the thought of them getting hurt because of her.

She was glad someone knew what was going on. She jerked at the sound of his voice when Parker came back into the room.

"I found some beer, which tastes so much better than coffee and made me some sandwiches. Want some?" he asked then laughed uproariously as if he had just told the greatest joke in the world. He filled his mouth. Debbie looked away from him. The sight of him eating was making her feel ill.

Debbie was glad she'd gone to bed with her watch on. She watched as the minutes ticked by, and then as those minutes turned into hours. Her captor was slowly making his way through the beer in the fridge, but she could tell he was getting restless. He kept looking at his own watch and frowning at it as if it had stopped working. He got up again, and she had to bite her lip to stop the nervous giggle forming in her throat from escaping. He was drunk. He was swaying on his feet as he made yet another trip to the kitchen. He must have gone through the six-pack of beer, because he began cursing and she could hear him pulling things from the fridge and dropping them on the floor.

He staggered back into the room and glared at her. "Where's the rest of the liquor?"

"Over in that cupboard," Debbie replied, indicating with a nod of her head the cabinet on the far side of the room against the wall. She hoped like hell he drained every drop of alcohol in the place. He would eventually fall into a drunken stupor if he did, and then maybe Remy could come in and set her free.

She saw him pull out a bottle of whiskey. He took the cap off and drank straight from the bottle.

"Don't think I'm going to pass out. I've always been able to hold my liquor," he said and belched. "Where the fuck are they? They should have been here by now. What were they going in for?"

"I don't know. When I woke up they were already gone."

"Stupid bitch," he muttered then took another swig.

Debbie glanced at her watch and saw it was nearly three o'clock. Her men should have been back hours ago, but she was glad they weren't here. She hoped that Remy had contacted them and were trying to think up a plan to get her out safely. She also hoped they stayed out of harm's way.

* * * *

Britt looked at his watch and cursed. He and Daniel had been away from home much longer than he'd anticipated. They were working in the sheriff's office with Luke and Damon. He was just glad that Remy had volunteered to watch over Debbie while he was not at home. His cell phone rang, and he felt his stomach sink when he saw who was calling.

"Remy, what's up? What? Fuck. Okay, we're on our way." He ended the call and turned to his brother. "That motherfucker is in the house and has Debbie tied to a chair with enough explosives on her to blow the whole goddamn block."

"How the fuck did he get in past the security system and Remy?" Daniel asked in a roar.

"I don't know, but we'll find out. Let's go. Luke, Damon, I want you as backup, but don't let him see you or your cars. We can get inside without him knowing about it," Britt bit out.

Britt felt sick to his stomach. To know the woman he loved was in the hands of some sick bastard made his guts churn, and his chest felt tight. He had to get himself under control. Letting his emotions rule could blow this, but his woman was in danger.

He pulled the truck up two houses down and jumped out. He took a few deep breaths and called on all of his training. Beside him, Daniel, too, was trying to calm down.

He worked his way to the house, keeping amongst the shadows so he wouldn't be seen. Daniel was at his heels. He snuck up behind Remy and smiled because the man had no idea he was there.

Crouching beside Remy near the living-room windows, he covered the other man's mouth with his hand. He didn't want Parker to be alerted to their presence if Remy yelled in fright.

"It's me," he whispered into Remy's ear and removed his hand. "Tell me what you've got."

"Shit," Remy whispered back. "You scared the crap outta me. He's got her tied to an armchair and in handcuffs. She's wearing a life jacket, which is covered with plastic explosives. He's halfway through your beer. I've been waiting for him to finish it so I could go in. He's going to be drunk by the time he finishes your stash."

"No. We can't take the chance he may have a remote detonator. Daniel and I will go in and he won't even know we're there."

He knew the other man was wondering why he hadn't seen Britt or his brother approach. He wanted, no, needed to get into the house to make sure his woman was all right. He hated that he had no control over the situation. Well, not as yet anyway, but he would soon.

"You stay here," Britt told Remy then muttered to his brother. "Let's go."

He made his way around to the back door, keeping on the balls of his feet. Every muscle in his body worked to prevent even the slightest noise. He cautiously opened the back door and slipped inside. Neither he nor Daniel made a sound. He moved stealthily down the hallway and peered into the living room. He could see the back of Debbie's head, and she moved marginally. The fear and anxiety in his gut lessened slightly at the sight of his unharmed love.

Fury rose in his body when he saw Parker walk back into the room. He was a big man, nearly as big as Daniel, and the thought of that bastard having his hands on Debbie nearly made him lose his control. He quickly pushed his feelings aside and silently moved farther into the room. He and his brother were going to have to wait. Britt needed to know if the fucker had a remote, and he wasn't willing to put his woman's life in danger by taking the sick prick down too early.

He listened as he asked for more liquor, and then the prick extolled his own prowess at being able to handle his drink, taunting his woman with the gun in his hand. Britt knew he was rattled by the way he kept looking at his watch. He wanted to grab the gun and shoot the bastard with it, but still he waited. For all he knew he could have the detonator in his pocket. He couldn't risk shooting the asshole and then having him push that button, if it existed, before he died.

"You're not going to get away with this. They will kill you," Debbie goaded.

Shit. Britt was going to spank her ass after he got her out of this.

"Now, that's where you're wrong, princess," he said. Britt watched as Parker placed the nearly empty bottle of whiskey on the coffee table, then reached into his pocket. "See this little button here?" Parker taunted. "One push and *ka-boom.*"

Britt felt the acid in his stomach churn. There was no way in hell he could jump the fucker now. His first priority was getting Debbie out of there safe and sound. He saw her shudder and wanted to be able to take her into his arms and comfort her, but if he revealed his presence, she might inadvertently give him and Daniel away. With visible effort, Debbie controlled her shuddering. "You don't have to do this," she said. "My men told me about your family. Maybe it's not too late—"

Parker cut her off. "This isn't about my family," he spat. "Prison taught me a few things, sweetheart. People don't matter." He turned toward the windows, drinking deeply from the bottle in his hand. Britt calculated the time it would take to leap across the room and incapacitate him.

But Daniel caught his eye and shook his head fractionally. The message was clear, and Britt knew it himself. The button might be back in Parker's pocket, but it was too dangerous to surprise him.

"What matters," Parker went on in a low voice, "is control. Like the way I've been controlling you for the past few weeks. You've been so afraid, and 'your men,' as you call them, have been running around in circles trying to figure out what's happening. They don't know I was the one who broke into your shop. They don't know I started the fire, either."

Britt shifted his gaze to Debbie. She was staring at Parker's back in open surprise. "You robbed me?" The rage built up in her voice almost at once. "You tried to kill me!"

"I was just having fun, sweetheart," Parker sneered. Britt prayed to God he would pass out soon. He was swaying on his feet, his skin looked pasty white, and as he turned to look at Debbie, Britt saw that his face was dotted with sweat. "I wanted to get them nice and worked up before I killed them. And besides, I enjoy a challenge. The security system here was a nice exercise of my training."

Britt exchanged another look with Daniel as Debbie asked, "Training?"

"Why yes." Parker slumped down onto the sofa near Debbie. He looked like he was having trouble keeping his eyes open. "Didn't 'your men' tell you? I trained with them. We spent years together learning how to protect this country, but I knew I was destined for greater things." He paused to lift the bottle to his lips again. "I'm so looking forward to this reunion."

He was so close to passing out, Britt thought. He made himself wait just a little longer. Already Parker's eyes were slipping shut. The hand around the liquor bottle slackened.

Britt stood perfectly still, breathing shallowly so he couldn't be heard. He watched and waited for what seemed like hours until finally Parker's eyelids closed for the final time.

Britt glanced to his brother long enough for Daniel to sign, *"Get the detonator."* He nodded and stepped out of the shadows.

Debbie's face turned toward them as they came into view. Britt registered her surprised expression, but he went to the couch first. Parker was so drunk and relaxed now that the hand holding the detonator was open. He plucked it up and placed it in his pocket. He flipped Parker over and cuffed him. The man didn't even stir.

He glanced up at Debbie and saw the tears in her eyes as she looked at him. Daniel got her out of the cuffs and rope and pulled the explosive jacket from her body. Britt picked up his cell and called Luke and Damon in to get Parker, and then he tapped on the window, signaling Remy. When Britt turned back to Debbie, he saw that Daniel had gathered her in his arms.

It was over, and their woman was safe.

Chapter Fifteen

Debbie clutched at Daniel as he picked her up from the armchair and into his arms. He and Britt had materialized out of thin air. Their bodies had seemed to emerge from the shadows. She was glad her men had such abilities and were there to rescue her.

Now that she was safe and not wrapped in explosives, reaction set in. She couldn't stop shaking and shivering, and even her teeth were chattering. Britt looked at her, and then he turned away. She knew that he felt guilty she been held hostage, and she would deal with that later, but right now she needed to get her body back in control. She heard footsteps entering the house and cringed, hiding her face against Daniel's neck.

"It's all right, honey, you're safe now. It's Luke, Damon, and Remy. Shh, Deb, you're fine," Daniel crooned.

Debbie felt tears prick her eyes, and then she sobbed against him. She clutched Daniel's shirt in her hands and cried her heart out. She had never been so scared in her life. She felt as if she had just looked death in the face.

Finally her crying slowed to only the occasional hiccup. She slumped on Daniel, her body relaxing for the first time in hours. She was so tired, and she felt like she could sleep for a week.

She released Dan's shirt and wiped her hands over her face then sat up. She was in his lap on the armchair she'd been tied to. His arms loosened, and she looked up to see concern on his face as he watched her in turn.

"I'm sorry."

"Shh, honey. You have nothing to be sorry for," Daniel replied.

"I got your shirt all wet."

"Honey, do you think I care about my shirt? God, you can cry on me anytime, Debbie. I love you. It killed me to see you so scared."

"I'm okay. I knew you and Britt would save me. God, I need a drink. Do we have any more whiskey?"

"Here you go, baby," Britt said. Debbie took the glass from his hand and downed the contents in one go. She gasped as the alcohol burned a path down her esophagus and hit her stomach. It warmed her from the inside out.

"Thanks," Debbie said and looked up at Britt. He looked so damn remorseful, and she knew he was blaming himself for what she'd been through. "It wasn't your fault."

"Yes, it was. We should never have left you alone. I can't believe I was so stupid," Britt said.

"You didn't leave me alone. The alarm was on and you sent Remy to watch over me," Debbie replied.

"Yeah, like that made a difference," Britt stated with anger directed at himself. "He still got past Remy and the alarm."

Debbie didn't want him to blame himself, but something Parker had said came back to mind. "How did he do that?" she asked.

She caught one of those looks passing between the brothers. "It's like he said," Britt admitted. He shook his head bitterly. "He was trained the same way we were. We should have known that there was no way to keep him from where he wanted to go." Overcome with anger, he turned away.

Debbie looked to Daniel for an explanation. "Parker never saw things our way," he said. "He sees his abilities and his training as an excuse to hurt people, not protect them." He looked past her. Debbie followed his gaze and found that the sheriffs were hauling an insensible Parker from the room at that moment. He was still out cold. "He never knew his own limits, either," Daniel added.

"That's something else we should have known." Britt's bitter tone made Debbie look toward him. He stood at the window where Parker himself had been only minutes before. His glare looked furious enough to melt the glass. "We should have known. We should have protected you better."

"Britt, stop it. I knew Remy was there. I saw him, and that made me feel a bit safer. I knew you and Daniel would come for me. I knew you would save me. Stop berating yourself for something which was completely out of your control," Debbie said with frustration. "If you had been here you would probably be dead. He was after you two in the first place. If he killed you, then where would I be? Things worked out this way for a reason. Just be thankful you were able to rescue me. I know I am. Thank you both so much for saving my life. I love you and want to spend the rest of my life with you."

"Are you asking us to marry you, honey?" Daniel asked and smiled at her.

Debbie smiled back. She had known if she got out of the situation with Parker alive, she was going to grab hold of her men and never let go. Life was too short to worry about getting hurt. She loved Britt and Daniel so much and needed them to be with her for the rest of her life. She wanted to marry them, have their children, and grow old with them. She was so excited to be with them and intended to spend the rest of her life showing them how much she loved them.

"Well, yeah, I guess I am," Debbie replied.

"Baby. God, I love you so much," Britt rasped and plucked her from Daniel's lap up into his arms. He hugged her fiercely, and even though it was a little uncomfortable, she didn't tell him to ease up. She wrapped her arms around his neck, her legs around his waist, and clung to him just as tightly.

"Does that mean you'll marry me?"

"Yes, baby. A thousand yeses. No one is going to get to you again," Britt declared emotionally.

Debbie lifted her head from his shoulder, cupped his cheek in her hand, and kissed him. She lost herself in his touch and taste. She never wanted to let him go. She moaned into his mouth as his tongue tangled with hers and then she felt Daniel at her back. He shifted her hair aside, hugging her from behind, and kissed along the back of her neck. She gentled the kiss and lifted her head. She stared into Britt's blue eyes and knew she was where she wanted and was meant to be. Sandwiched between her two shadow men.

The next few hours were busy with giving statements to Luke and Damon. Her two men stayed by her side, holding her hands and offering her comfort. Telling the two sheriffs about the ordeal brought up all her anxiety, so she kept herself busy. She brewed coffee, cleaned up the mess on the floor Parker had made, and cooked a pot of chili. By the time they all left, Debbie wanted to shower and fall into bed. She was so tired now she could barely stand.

She was thankful for Britt and Daniel's help in the bathroom, and then Britt carried her to bed. Between her two men again, she snuggled up to Britt as Daniel cuddled her from behind. But sleep eluded her. She was restless and couldn't seem to settle.

"Are you okay, honey?" Daniel murmured against her ear.

"Yes. No. I don't know. I can't get my mind to shut off."

"Do you want us to take your mind off things? We can make you feel good, baby," Britt said quietly.

"You don't have to," Debbie replied.

"We know that, honey, but we want to. Just lie back, close your eyes, and let us pleasure you," Daniel rumbled.

Daniel eased Debbie onto her back, leaned over, and gently kissed her. She knew he was holding back from her, because his kisses were usually more dominant and carnal. She was glad he was being careful of her, but she didn't want that right now. She lifted her arms and clutched at his hair with her hands. She tightened her grip and pulled his mouth harder against hers. He certainly got the message. He let go and began to kiss her in earnest. His tongue swept into her mouth, tangling it with hers, and then he withdrew and nipped her lower lip. He took one of her breasts in his hand and kneaded her flesh. She arched up against him and groaned into his mouth when he began rubbing his thumb over her nipple.

Debbie mewled when she felt Britt kissing his way down her torso and over her stomach. He nudged her legs apart with his hands. She shifted as the mattress dipped and he was now between her thighs. She sobbed with frustration as Daniel removed his mouth from hers, and then she cried out as he sucked her turgid peak into his mouth.

She thrust her hips up when Britt ran his tongue through her moist labia and flicked it over her clit. Her pussy clenched, begging to be filled, and her sensitive bundle of nerves throbbed. Britt gently pushed two fingers into her pussy. She keened and reached down to clutch his head to her.

"Easy, baby. Just relax, we'll give you what you need," Britt growled out. She whimpered when he began pumping his fingers in and out of her cunt as he lapped over her clit and Daniel sucked on one nipple while pinching the other. Liquid heat traveled from her breasts down to her belly to pool in her womb and pussy. She loved how her two men made her feel and knew she would never be able to get enough of them.

She moved her hand to Daniel's stomach and slid it down until she found his cock. She fisted him and began to pump along the length of his shaft. He groaned against her breast, sending ripples of vibration into her. Her muscles were beginning to quiver, and she was starting to climb the pinnacle toward ecstasy. She bucked her hips up and cried out as Britt's digits ran over her G-spot. He slurped against her flesh, and then he sucked her clit into his mouth.

Debbie screamed as her internal walls clamped down around his fingers and she flew into the sky. Neither of her men stopped pleasuring her until the last wave of her climax faded away. She gasped in a breath and flopped down on the bed, her limbs heavy and replete from her orgasm.

Her men drew up beside her, pulled the covers over her, and cuddled close to her again. She felt tears prick her eyes at the unselfish way they had just loved her, and she knew even though they must be aching, they weren't going to push her to relieve them. Well, she loved them too much, and she was having none of that, because she wanted to feel them inside her. She felt so connected to them when they loved her together. It felt as if they touched each other's souls.

Debbie squirmed and rolled until she was in the perfect spot. She took Britt's cock in hand and sucked him into her mouth. She smiled around his flesh when she heard him moan.

"Baby, you don't have to do that. We know how tired you are."

Debbie pulled her mouth from his cock to answer. "I know. I want to. I love you both so much. I need to do this. Please, just let me." She lowered her head again and took him into the depths of her mouth. He was so big she could have wrapped both her fists around the flesh she couldn't get into her mouth. She bobbed up and down his length, gliding her hand around the remainder of his dick. She took him as deep as she could without gagging and slid back up again. She swirled her tongue around the corona of his cock and then laved the sensitive underside. She moaned when she felt him jerk in her hand.

She reached over, feeling her way to find Daniel, and then gripped his cock in her free hand. She pumped up and down his shaft and was rewarded when he groaned. Debbie wanted to finish what she'd started, but she also wanted them inside her, together. She let go of Daniel, licked the length of Britt's erection, and pushed the covers back from over her head. She blinked in the light from the bedside lamp, and then she began to crawl up over Britt. She sat on his thighs and held her hand out to Daniel. When he took hers, she looked at him and back to Britt, pleading to them with her eyes.

"Come here, baby," Britt murmured. She sighed as he clasped her hips in his big hands and helped to move her. She reached down and held his cock at the entrance to her pussy. She kept her eyes on his as she slowly sank down on him.

"Fuck, you feel so good, baby. So hot and wet and tight," he growled out.

"So do you. You fill me so good. I love you, Britt. I love you, Daniel," she declared, looking at them each in turn.

"Tell us what you want, baby," Daniel said, stroking her back.

She didn't even have to think about her answer. "I want you in my ass."

"Are you sure, honey?"

"I've never been so sure of anything in my life. Please?"

"Okay, Deb. Lie down on Britt and let me prepare you," Daniel said, and his deep, gravelly voice told Debbie he wanted to love her, too.

She obeyed his command and lay over Britt. She sighed as he wrapped his arms around her and kissed the top of her head.

"A little cold lube, honey," Daniel warned.

Debbie held still and concentrated on keeping her muscles loose. She moaned as Daniel massaged the sensitive skin of her ass, and then he pushed into her. She breathed evenly and deeply, trying to stay relaxed for him. He pressed through her tight sphincter, and then he slid his digits in and out a few times.

"Good girl. You're doing great, honey," Daniel crooned. He withdrew his fingers, and she heard the tube of lube pop. Then the liquid sounds penetrated her ears. He was coating his cock with the gel.

"Just stay still, Deb," Daniel whispered as he covered her back with his body.

She groaned as the flesh of her anus burned slightly and pinched as Daniel eased into her. Once he was past the tight ring of muscles, he slid in easily.

"Fuck, honey. You're so hot and tight," Daniel gasped. "Let me help you up, Deb."

Debbie sighed as Daniel moved off her back and pulled her with him. When he had her sitting on his cock with her body perpendicular to the mattress, Britt sat up, too. She was so full of cock, and they were in her body as far as they could go. She reached out and clutched at Britt's massive biceps. She straddled Daniel with her legs hooked around his arms, Britt's hands at her hips to help hold her, and both her men bore her weight.

"Are you ready, baby?" Britt asked breathlessly.

Debbie couldn't find her voice, so she nodded. Then she moaned. They loved on her at the same time. They rocked, held her up, and thrust their hips at her, their cocks sliding in and out of her holes. She wanted them to go faster and tried to wriggle her hips.

"Let us do all the work, honey," Daniel panted out around a groan.

They were going too slow. She needed all of them. She needed them to love her hard and fast, to wipe out the memories of a nightmare of a day.

"Fuck me," Debbie sobbed. "I need you to fuck me hard."

"We don't want to hurt you, baby," Britt sighed. She could hear the tightness of his voice as he kept himself under control.

"You would never hurt me. Please, I need you. Faster, harder. Fuck me," Debbie pleaded.

Her words snapped their control, and they pounded in and out of her ass and pussy. She was so close. The friction of their cocks shuttling in and out of her body heated her from the inside out and sent pleasurable ripples running through her. She closed her eyes and gasped for breath as she felt the coils begin to tighten. Her limbs shook, and she dug her nails into Britt's flesh. Tighter and tighter the spring wound, her body gathering in on itself, hurtling toward its culmination.

She screamed as those internal coils snapped. Stars formed before her closed eyelids, and she threw her head back as her body shuddered. The walls of her pussy and ass clamped and released as waves of pleasure consumed her. She was vaguely aware of her men yelling as they followed her over the cliff into nirvana.

Debbie opened her eyes when she felt a warm cloth between her legs. She sighed and snuggled up to Daniel. She wriggled her hips but stilled when Britt got into bed and cuddled up to her back. Her body began to relax, and she savored being surrounded by the men. She was wrapped up in so much love and warmth. She felt happy, content, and secure. She was going to treasure every moment she had with her men.

Epilogue

Debbie had been so busy planning all week, and when the day finally dawned she was fraught with nerves. She had invited all the people of Slick Rock who were involved in ménage relationships to the barbecue, as well as the Alcott brothers. She had been looking forward to the day, and she was nearly ready. She could hear the guests outside talking and laughing and knew they didn't have a clue about the events that were to take place in a few moments.

Debbie took one last look at her dress and smiled. She didn't look half bad, even if she said so herself. She had made her dress, and of course it was in a light shade of her favorite color. It was a simple dress, with shoestring straps and layered mauve silk which ended at her ankles. She'd left her hair long, falling to her waist in rippling waves, and only had on the lightest touches of makeup. There was a discreet knock on the door, and it opened to reveal Remy Alcott. He was dressed in slacks and a shirt but no tie, which was just the way she wanted it. She hadn't wanted people to have to fuss and worry about what to wear. It was going to be informal, and only friends had been invited.

"You look gorgeous, sugar. Are you ready?

"Yes."

"Okay then let's get this show on the road," Remy said nervously.

Debbie wrapped her arm around Remy's and let him guide her to the back door, which stood wide open. She saw him give a nod of his head and the music began. The music and lyrics of "The Way You Make Me Feel" by Ronan Keating drifted through the air. She stepped into view of the doorway and saw faces turn toward her with surprise and then delight. The marriage officiator stood waiting in the landscaped gardens of the backyard, just beyond the rose-covered archway. She saw her men move into position beneath the arch, and her breath caught in her throat.

They looked so handsome in their black trousers and mauve shirts. She held their gazes as Remy led her down the gravel path toward her future. Reaching them, she thanked Remy and took Britt's and Daniel's hands in hers and faced the celebrant.

The ceremony was short but so full of love and emotion she couldn't stop the tears from falling. The scent of white iceberg roses permeated the air as she became Mrs. Debbie Delaney. She kissed Britt and then turned to Daniel and kissed him as well. On paper she was married to Britt, but in her heart and theirs, she was married to both of them.

"I present to you Mr. and Mrs. Delaney."

A cheer went up, and everyone began to clap. Debbie was swept up in congratulations, standing between the loves of her life, as her guests kissed her and her men shook hands. The Alcott brothers manned the grill, and champagne was poured. They ate, drank, and laughed. They all celebrated well into the night, and by the time the last guest left, Debbie was still walking on clouds.

She turned toward her men, and then she laughed as she was swept from her feet. They both carried her over the threshold and managed to get through the doorway together without breaking their hold. She was looking forward to the next fifty or so years with her husbands by her side. But for now they were going to do some of their own private celebrating.

THE END

WWW.BECCAVAN-EROTICROMANCE.COM

ABOUT THE AUTHOR

My name is Becca Van. I live in Australia with my wonderful hubby of many years, as well as my two children.

I read my first romance at the age of thirteen, which I found in the school library, and haven't stopped reading them since. It is so wonderful to know that love is still alive and strong when there seems to be so much conflict in the world.

I dreamt of writing my own book one day but unfortunately, didn't follow my dream for many years. But once I started I knew writing was what I wanted to continue doing.

I love to escape from the world and curl up with a good romance, to see how the characters unfold and conflict is dealt with. I have read many books and love all facets of the romance genre, from historical to erotic romance. I am a sucker for a happy ending.

Also by Becca Van

Ménage Everlasting: Slick Rock 1: *Slick Rock Cowboys*
Ménage Everlasting: Slick Rock 2: *Double E Ranch*
Ménage Everlasting: Slick Rock 3: *Her Ex-Marines*
Ménage Everlasting: Slick Rock 4: *Leah's Irish Heroes*
Ménage Everlasting: Slick Rock 6: *Her Personal Security*

For all other titles, please visit
www.bookstrand.com/becca-van

Siren Publishing, Inc.
www.SirenPublishing.com

Lightning Source UK Ltd.
Milton Keynes UK
UKOW06f1856160816

280854UK00019B/414/P